RAT

RAT

Jan Cheripko

Boyds Mills Press

The actual act of writing appears on the surface to be the work of one person. I doubt that that is completely true. But surely the act of getting a book into the hands of readers is not accomplished by the efforts of only one person. So I offer my sincere thanks for the help of many: Kent Brown, Clay Winters, Larry Rosler, Tim Gillner, and all the great people at Boyds Mills Press; Marcia Marshall, my editor, who pressed me and guided me to get to the story; Neil Waldman, my friend, who took my words and put a face to them; to Felipe Lopez, Christine Spiecher, Janet Allen, Frank Hodge, Evelyn Rivers, and Anne Cobb, who read the work early on and encouraged me; to my dear friends Tom White, Mike Ducey, and Chris Stein, who have always encouraged me; to the staff and students at The Family Foundation School, who give a reason to write; to a special friend, Andrea Bown, who exemplifies the word *courage*; and to my wife, Val, and daughter, Julia, who teach me more each day about love.

YOUR LOVE HAS LIFTED ME (HIGHER & HIGHER)
Words and Music by GARY JACKSON, CARL SMITH, and RAYNARD MINER
© 1967 CHEVIS MUSIC, INC., WARNER-TAMERLANE PUBLISHING CORP
and UNICHAPPELL MUSIC INC. (Renewed)
All Rights Reserved Used by Permission
Warner Bros. Publications U.S. Inc., Miami, Florida 33014

Published by Boyds Mills Press, Inc.
A Highlights Company
815 Church Street
Honesdale, Pennsylvania 18431
Printed in China
Visit our Web site at www.boydsmillspress.com

Publisher Cataloging-in-Publication Data

Cheripko, Jan.
Rat / by Jan Cheripko. — 1st ed.
[224] p. : col. Ill. ; cm.
Summary: A fifteen-year-old with a love of basketball realizes telling the truth may sometimes have unanticipated consequences in this coming-of-age novel.
ISBN 1-59078-034-5
1. Basketball—Fiction—Juvenile literature. 2. Adolescence—Fiction—Juvenile literature. [1. Basketball—Fiction. 2. Adolescence—Fiction.]
I. Title.
813.54 [F] 21 CIP 2002
2002103218

First edition, 2002
The text of this book is set in 12.5 New Century Schoolbook.

10 9 8 7 6 5 4 3 2 1

To my father, John, and my mother, Frances—
may I bring you some small
token of honor and hope for peace

—J. C.

CHAPTER ONE

"WHAT DID SHE SAY?"

I didn't answer right away, so the lawyer said again, "What did Cassandra Diaz say when you entered the room?"

I looked out into the courtroom. I could see the basketball players all sitting together staring at me. All I could think of was the fact that my tie was too tight. I shouldnta let my mother tie it. I shoulda done it myself.

"Mr. Chandler," the judge was saying to me now, "you have to answer the question. What did Ms. Diaz say when you entered the room?"

It all came down to me sayin' what I saw. I couldn't lie. My mother told me I couldn't. My father insisted that I didn't. The lawyer warned me and coached me. And really I didn't want to lie, because I know what I saw. But none of them had to face the basketball team. None of them were gonna have to go through what I would face in school after this day.

"Can I have a glass of water, ma'am?" I asked the judge.

"Sure," she smiled. "Bailiff, please get Mr. Chandler a glass of water."

It didn't take long to get me the water. I took a sip. "Now, Mr. Chandler," urged the judge.

"Well, ma'am—"

"I'd like you to speak to the jury," she said.

I slid in my seat, like I used to on the tall kitchen chairs at home, usually knocking over a glass of soda or my cereal bowl, getting my mom to yell at me. My eyes slid, too, right across every eyeball in their basketball heads: Josh, Felipe, Greg, Ryley, Niko, Leduane, Paul, Jordan, and the worst of them at the end, Simpson.

"Cass didn't say anything," I said to the jury.

"She didn't say anything?" the lawyer asked, just like we had rehearsed.

"No, sir," I said.

"What did Ms. Diaz do?"

"She looked at me."

"What kind of look?"

"It was a sad look, like she needed help," I said.

"Objection!" yelled the other lawyer. "That's purely interpretation—"

"He's the only witness, your honor, he's got to be—" the prosecutor was saying.

"He can witness what he saw, your honor, but he can't interpret it."

"Sustained," said the judge.

"Your honor—" said the prosecutor.

"I said, 'sustained,'" she repeated. Then she turned to me, "Answer the question by describing exactly what you saw."

"Well, Coach Stennard was pressing her up against the wall in his office. Cass's hands were on his shoulders, trying to push him away. He was breathin' heavy and was tryin' to kiss her on the mouth."

"Objection, he can't know for sure if the defendant was trying to kiss her."

"Overruled. I have a feeling this young man knows a kiss when he sees one."

I wasn't sure I knew what she meant by sayin' that. If she meant 'cause I'd been kissed a lot or kissed girls a lot, well, she was wrong. A lot of older girls told me I was cute, even Cass did once, but I never kissed a girl. Not really. Wanted to, and I'm fifteen, so I suppose I should have by now, but there haven't been many girls willing to kiss a guy with a withered arm. Not the way I wanted, anyway.

"Continue, young man."

"Well, Coach was trying to kiss her and everything."

9

"What does, 'and everything' mean?"

"Well, you know. Like he was pressin' on her and had his hands all over her."

"Where were his hands?"

"Well, you know, up here, on here," I said putting my hands near my chest, "on her buzzas."

There was a loud roar of laughter in the courtroom. Even the prosecutor was smiling, trying not laugh right along with everyone else. I guess I had forgotten that part of the coaching about what to call a girl's chest.

"You mean breasts?"

"Yeah."

"What did Mr. Stennard say when he saw you?"

"He said, 'Rat, don't you have some job to do?'"

"And you said?"

" 'Yes sir, I do.' But I didn't leave."

"Why not?"

"Because I knew what was happening wasn't right."

"Why not?"

"Because, like I said, Cass looked at me like she didn't want to be there. And Coach looked at me like he hated me."

"Interpretation, your honor!" cried the other lawyer.

"Overruled. It's clear the young man could read body language and facial expressions."

"Your honor—" the other lawyer was saying.

"Overruled, I said," answered the judge. "You can address your objections in your cross-examination."

The prosecutor continued. But just like we had rehearsed, he changed his questions.

"By the way, Jeremy, why do they call you Rat?"

"That's a nickname. I had it for years, 'cause I'm always in the gym playin' ball. So they call me a gym rat. Rat for short."

"You like playing basketball?"

"Oh yeah. I love it. Course, I'm not all that great, because of my arm," I said, looking down at my withered stump of an arm. "But I'm fast, and I can dribble and shoot pretty good, so I do all right."

This was all so the prosecutor could play on the sympathy of the jury. Make me out to be like a really good kid with a bad arm. Sometimes I think I'm a really bad kid with one good arm and one arm I can use to get what I want. Doesn't always work. My mom's wise to me. I s'pose Dad is, too.

"And because you like basketball, you became manager of the team?"

"Yes, sir."

"And as manager you could come and go as you like, even into the coach's office?"

"Yeah, I s'pose. Never thought about that much. I always had to get stuff like balls, tape, shoelaces."

"Why did you go into the coach's office on the day in question?"

"I wanted one of the good game balls to shoot with. The season was over, so I didn't figure anyone would mind me usin' a good ball."

"And when you walked in and saw Mr. Stennard with Ms. Diaz, and he told you to leave and then you didn't, what happened then?"

"He yelled at me to get my 'F"in' ass out of his office or he'd beat the 'S' out of me. Do I have to say those words, sir? My mom wouldn't like it."

More laughter.

"No. No you don't. That's fine. What did you do then?"

"I just stood there."

"Why didn't you leave?"

"I was too scared to move."

"What then happened?"

"Coach reached over to pick up something from the desk. I think maybe it was a stapler, to throw at me. When he reached over Cass pulled away from him and yelled, "Let me go!" Coach Stennard grabbed at her, but she was out of his hold."

"Did you get a good look at Ms. Diaz as she left?"

"Yes."

"What did you notice?"

"She was crying and her bloused was ripped open."

"Then what did you do?"

"I turned around to look at Coach Stennard."

"And what did he do?"

"He looked right into my eyes."

"Did he say anything to you?"

"Yes."

"Will you please tell the court what he said?"

"'You breath one word of this to anyone, you little bastard, and I'll slit your throat.'"

CHAPTER TWO

MY MOM MAKES THE BEST MASHED POTATOES of anyone I know. Thick, with tons of butter melting all over them. They're my favorite. But do you know how hard it is to swallow when you have to face a school full of people who hate your guts? Everyone—that is, lots of adults—were telling me what a great job I did on the witness stand. Big deal. So now I sit at dinner starin' at mashed potatoes that look like a blob of white paste and taste about the same, my mom and dad starin' at me like they can't figure out what to say. And neither can I.

Coach Stennard was found guilty for attempted rape, assault, battery, unlawful imprisonment, and endangering the welfare of a minor. I don't know whether I was the minor or Cass was. Maybe we both were. The sentencing was set for sometime in

February, about four months away. Coach Stennard was out on bail, but he didn't live near town, so I didn't figure I'd run into him at all. At the end of the trial, the judge told the court that I was a hero. Simpson and the others didn't think so. When I walked by him, he said, "You're gonna wish you were never born, 'buzza' Rat."

"It'll take time, Jeremy," Mom was sayin', "but they'll forget, and it'll work out in the end."

"I'm going to drive you to school tomorrow," my dad said.

"No, it's okay, Dad. I can take the bus."

"I know you can, but I've got some time, and I'd like to drive you."

I think maybe that was a bit of a lie. My dad's a doctor, and he doesn't have much time at all. But maybe it wasn't a lie. Maybe he's got time because he's takin' time. I admire my dad. A lot of people admire him. They admire him so much, they elected him president of the school board. He's really honest and fair. But he's not a guy you warm up to. He's just not a huggy kind of guy. Which is okay, I guess. He's not the kinda guy to say, "I love you." And to tell you the truth, I didn't really want to get on that bus tomorrow, anyway.

I knew there were going to be plenty of kids who were going to call me names. There already were before the trial. I was getting used to it. I thought I had friends, but it didn't seem like I did now. Most of my friends were on the basketball team. I mean, I know, 'cause of my arm, I was only like a mascot to them. I mean, I'm not blind. But I did think that some of them were really my friends. They were guys I looked up to. And now they hated me. If I thought too much on that, I'd just start cryin'. I did the first time all this mess started and they found out that I saw Coach with Cass, and that I had told my parents about it and my parents had told the principal.

Well, when all that came out, the basketball players had a meeting and I was the center of it. I mean literally. They stood me in the middle of the locker room and wanted to know what I was going to say and what I'd already said. So I told them the truth, because that's what I saw.

"That really sucks," said Felipe.

"I know," I said. "Coach shouldnta done that."

"I don't mean Coach, asshole! I mean you. What you did. What you said. That sucks."

It was like he kicked me in my stomach. I couldn't breathe. I couldn't believe what I was hearing. I thought I was doing the right thing, and here Felipe and the others were tellin' me that I was wrong. How could I be wrong? I didn't do anything. Coach did!

"What are we gonna do?" asked Leduane.

And that's when Simpson stepped in.

"We aren't gonna do anything," he said, as he walked up to me. "You, Rat, are gonna do it all."

"Whaddya mean, Simp?" I said.

"You're gonna go back to the principal, the prosecutor, and your parents and tell them that you lied. That you made this whole thing up."

"I can't."

"Don't say you can't!" he screamed at me. "Don't say you can't. You will! You'll tell them you lied. And that's it."

"Well, you still got the problem of Cass," said Josh.

"Screw her!" Simpson turned on Josh. "It'll be her word against Coach's. Everyone knows that she's a slut. She'd do anyone."

"Right, Simp," said Greg. "You ever screw her? No, I didn't think so. That's not one you're going to get to stick."

"It will if we all say it. We'll just tell everyone that she screws the basketball team all the time. There's nine of us. Our word against that spic's."

Simpson must have realized what he had said, 'cause he looked quickly at Felipe. "No offense, Flip." Felipe didn't say anything, he just looked hard at Simpson, who turned back on me like a dog after a bone.

"You see what you've done, creep? You got us fighting."

Like that was my fault. But I was caught and there wasn't anything I could say to get out of it.

"Let him be." It was Josh again. "He can't change his story. What's done is done. They're not going to believe him anyway if he changes it."

"Whaddya mean? Whadda we gonna do?"

"Nothin'. Let it be."

So they let it be. That was back in March, after we had won the league championship but got knocked off in the first round of the sectional play-offs. We lost by eleven points to a team we had beaten easily during the regular season. We had coasted to the league title, and then got upset in the first round. It was a tough loss. But every single kid on that team was back for this coming season. That's what made the thing with Coach Stennard so bad. Everybody on the team, in the school, in the community, in the county, figured we'd be on our way to another league championship, to a sectional title, and maybe even to a state title.

Let me tell you how amazin' that would be. We're a really small school. Only twenty-eight kids in the graduating class. Usually, we're toward the bottom of the pile, even though we play in Class D, for small schools. But last year, like I said, we were undefeated in the league. And we only lost two games outside the league. One was to James Monroe, a Class B school, and we almost knocked off St. Vincent's, a Catholic school power. So we're really good. And like I said, everyone was back. Everyone except Coach Stennard. He's going to jail.

CHAPTER THREE

EVER SEE A DEAD RAT UP CLOSE? The eyes stick out at you like black headlights.

I know it was Simpson who hung it from my locker and wrote the sign above it that said, "The only good buzza rat is dead buzza rat!"

He was standin' in the back of a bunch of kids right by my locker. He's six foot three inches tall, with bleached-blond, short-cut hair. Hard to miss, so I knew he was behind this. I wanted to laugh to be brave, but I knew if I made a sound, I'd cry—or worse, puke. So I just turned and walked to homeroom, listening to them chant, "Buzza rat! Buzza rat! Buzza rat!"

I didn't go back to my locker all day long, which made life a little hard, because all my books and homework were in there. The only bright spot for most of the day was in earth science, where we have Mr. O'Connor. Now, you wouldn't think that earth science would be cool, but Mr. O'Connor, who just started at Sparrowburg in September of this year, makes it that way. He always has us acting out things that he's talking about. This time he had us pretending we were the airflows in a warm front as a cold front moved in.

"So the cold front moves in on top of the warm front," he's tellin' us, as he moves a few of us through the make-believe sky in the front of the room, "and when it hits the warm front there's lightning and thunder. *Bam! Bam! Crash!*"

Then he shows us a tub of water that was supposed to be the rain. "And when those two fronts hit and start fighting with each other . . ."

Now he picks up the tub of water, and we're lookin' at each other, thinkin', *This doesn't look good.*

". . . when they hit each other, then *bam*, a storm erupts," and he heaves the water at us.

But somehow he switched tubs and threw confetti all over us! It was neat. We were roaring so much that old Mr. Wallace, who teaches physics next door, came in to see what the commotion was all about.

"What is going on in here?" Mr. Wallace demanded.

"Change in the weather, Mr. Wallace," Mr.

O'Connor said, trying to be serious. "Cold front moving through. Bad storm. Baaaaad storm."

Like I said, that was about the only bright spot in the day, until after school.

I went down to the gym, because that's where I always hang out. I knew some of the basketball team would be there, but I figured that most of them, 'specially Josh, Felipe, Leduane, Greg, and I guess all the others, except Simpson, wouldn't really hurt me. They might call me names, but I love to play ball so much, that a few names weren't gonna keep me from it. And if Simpson was there, they wouldn't let him beat me. At least, that's what I hoped.

Josh and Felipe were lacing their sneakers. I said hello to them, and they both at least nodded their heads at me, even if they didn't say hello. A couple of the players from the girls' team were shooting down at the other end of the court.

Now, up until they took Coach Stennard from the courtroom in handcuffs, he was still technically a teacher here at Sparrowburg. He wasn't actually teachin'. He had been suspended with pay. My dad said that the board had to pay him, 'cause he wasn't yet found guilty. And up until that day, just yesterday, some people in town, most of the players anyway, figured he'd be coachin' the Bearcats this coming season. Either they didn't figure he had done anything wrong, or maybe they thought Cass was wrong. Which to me is really weird. I mean, I was there; Cass didn't do anything wrong.

Still, the basketball season started in just two days, and the best team in the league had no coach. They couldn't hire a new coach because, like I said, technically Coach Stennard hadn't done anything wrong. I know that the school board had been talking about it, but nobody knew, 'cause they always met in executive session. The newspapers tried to find out. They were callin' my dad all the time. Either tryin' to find out who the new coach would be or wantin' to talk to me. Which dad always said no to. So with two days to go, and Coach Stennard on his way to jail, the guys were getting ready to play no matter who the coach would be.

I walked over to where the two girls were shootin'. Megan Vanderstahl and Katie Callahan. Katie's a freshman, a year younger than me, and she's kinda cute. They're both starters on the girls' team and they're both pretty good. I picked up a ball and started to shoot. They didn't say anything, just looked at each other and walked down to the other end of the court to shoot at the other basket.

I swallowed hard to check myself from crying and put up a shot. *Swish! Well,* I thought, *at least I can still shoot.* Pretty soon I lost myself in a make-believe world I know how to create whenever I want to. I've been doing that for years. Ever since I was a little kid and other kids started to make fun of my withered stump of an arm. You get used to the names after a while. It doesn't matter. It's who you are; I mean, I'm a kid with crippled arm. Do I dream about not having a bad arm? Sure. But I don't know life without a withered arm, so it's just life.

But I always knew that anytime I wanted to, I could slip into my make-believe world. Basketball became part of it. But you know, one of my problems is that my withered arm is my right arm, and I'm right-handed. I tried to use my right hand just like everyone else. I couldn't, even though I wanted to. So I had to teach myself how to be left-handed.

I still remember my mom tryin' to teach me to write my letters when I was a little kid. She'd do it with her right hand, so I would try to do it with my right hand. Wasn't until she got someone who was left-handed—it was Josh's older sister, Melissa—that I finally started to figure this out.

But that's why I'm such a good shooter—because I have to concentrate so hard. I just don't miss.

So there I am shootin' the eyes out, when I see Simpson come into the gym. I know this isn't going to be pleasant.

"Oh, my God!" he says. "Do I smell somethin' stinkin' up this gym? Is it old socks? Why hell, no! It's a rat. A buzza rat! A dead buzza rat! Do you smell that?" he says, looking at Felipe and Josh.

"Let it alone," says Josh quietly.

"Let it alone? Hell, no! We can't have rats in our gym stinkin' up the place. Get your rotten rat ass outta here!" screams Simpson, as he throws a ball as hard as he can at me. His aim isn't very good, so I don't have to move at all, and the ball smashes into the door of the coach's room. The loud crash brings out Mrs. Pollard, who used to coach the girls' team but is now the cheerleading coach, and, of all people, Mr. O'Connor, just as Simpson yells at me, "Off the court, Rat! You got no right to be here."

"What's going on?" yells Mrs. Pollard.

"Sorry, I thought I saw a rat," says Simpson, sarcastically, as he turns back to Felipe and Josh.

Mr. O'Connor looks at me and then at Simpson. He picks up the ball and walks onto the court.

"You guys were undefeated in the league last year, right?"

The guys mumble yeah and nod their heads.

"Of course, you lost in the sectional playoffs," he says.

Felipe and Josh look at each other. Simpson scowls.

"Tell you what, Bart—"

"That's Simpson."

"Oh, pardon me, got you mixed up with someone else," says Mr. O'Connor, which brings a smile to Megan and Katie.

"Tell you what, Simpy, I'd like to see how good you guys are. Got time for a quick game?"

Simpson looks at Felipe and Josh, then back at Mr. O'Connor. "Sure," he says.

"You choose two, I choose two. Go ahead, pick your two first."

Simpson looks at him, like he's jokin'.

"Go ahead, Simpy, choose," says Mr. O'Connor.

"You really are a glutton for punishment," says Simpson.

"Maybe. Choose."

"Flip and Josh."

"I got the two girls."

This really pisses me off. I'm not better than these two girls? Still, this should be interesting. Three basketball players against two girls and a science teacher.

"You go first," says Mr. O'Connor to Simpson.

Now here's the lineups for you: Felipe—he's about five foot, eleven inches tall. Shoots well from the outside, fast, and very strong to the basket. Josh, also about five foot eleven. Tough as nails on defense and a very good jumper. And Simpson Theodore III, who we call Teddy Simpleton da Turd, or Simple Turd, or just Da Turd, but never to his face. He's six foot three, about two hundred and twenty pounds, strong as an ox, but the ox is smarter.

Against Megan Vanderstahl, who can shoot from

the outside, but isn't more than five foot five and not that quick; Katie Callahan, who can shoot even better than Megan, and she's quicker, and with her long brown hair and slender body, is a lot cuter. Course cute doesn't help in basketball. But she is cute. And Mr. O'Connor, who is about five foot eleven, weighs about a hundred and sixty pounds, and wears glasses.

"Here, hold these," he says to me, as he hands me his glasses. "I can't see a thing without them. Blondie," he says to Megan, "What's your name?"

"Megan Vanderstahl."

"Ah, Megan. A lovely name. Same name as me daughter's. Megan, you guard him," he says, pointing to Felipe. "And your name?"

"Katie Callahan."

"Ah, one o' me own kind, an Irish girl," he says with a fake Irish accent. "Okay, little Irish lass, Katie, you take the Josh man. And I'll take Bart here."

Simpson gives him an angry look. "Simpson."

"Right. I'll guard you. Your ball," he says, tossing it to Felipe. "Pass in. Make it, take it. Shooter calls the fouls. First one to eleven wins."

Well, I think to myself, *at least he talks a good game.*

Felipe passes in to Josh, who dribbles twice, and swishes a twelve-footer.

"A jumper from the Josh man," says Mr.

O'Connor, tossing the ball to Josh.

Josh passes to Felipe, who sinks a fifteen-footer.

"Oh, they're bringing the house down," sings Mr. O'Connor, tossing the ball again to Josh.

Megan goes up close to Felipe to challenge the jump shot, but he blows right by her like she was standing still for an easy lay-up.

"Three-nothin'," says Simpson, then he looks at me.

CHAPTER FOUR

THREE TO NOTHIN'. Looked to me like this wasn't gonna be much of a game. Josh passed to Felipe, and then the ball went to Simpson, who hoisted a shot from a foot behind the three-point line. It clanged off the base of the rim into Mr. O'Connor's hands.

"Oh, too bad, Bart. A brick."

By now Greg, Niko, and Ryley are out in the gym and so are a couple of kids from the girls' team. I can tell Simpson's gettin' mad. He comes out after Mr. O'Connor, who fakes the drive, pulls up, and sinks a shot well beyond the three-point arc.

"Three to one," says Mr. O'Connor.

Mr. O'Connor passes to Katie, who tries to pass back to Mr. O'Connor, but Josh steps in for the steal and then passes to Felipe down low. He puts in an easy lay-up.

"Four to one," says Simpson.

Felipe takes the ball out and inbounds to Simpson. He starts to drive, but Mr. O'Connor swats the ball away to Katie. She passes back to him and *swish*.

"Four-two," says Mr. O'Connor.

Megan passes in to Mr. O'Connor, who again fakes right and pulls up for the jumper—*swish*.

"Four-three, Barty boy."

"Com'on, Simpson, put a hand in his face. You got four inches on him," says Felipe.

Simpson pulls up the bottom of his shorts and squats down low, like he's ready to play some defense, but Mr. O'Connor fakes right again and zooms by him for an easy lay-up.

"Seems to be tied," he says, smiling.

Megan inbounds to him, he goes right this time, and Felipe steps in to cut off the drive. Bounce pass to Megan. Now, girls may not be as quick as guys, or as tall, or as strong, but if you leave them open for a shot, they'll drain the bottom of the net every time. *Swish*.

"Five-four, fellows," says Mr. O'Connor.

Next time, he kicks out to Katie, who banks home a twelve-footer when Josh drops off to cover Mr. O'Connor, 'cause Simpson can't come close to stayin' with him.

Megan takes the next shot, which bounces high

off the front of the rim, but Mr. O'Connor skies out of nowhere to tap it in.

"Seven to four. You guys better get serious," Mr. O'Connor says.

By now word about this game had spread, 'cause there's lots of kids standing on the sidelines and in the doorways. I can see Cass standin' in the back.

Mr. O'Connor takes the ball at the top of the key, looks over to Katie, motions a little with his head. She nods back and sets a screen for Megan, who goes backdoor on Felipe. A pinpoint pass under the basket for an easy lay-up.

A large cheer from the kids watching.

"Eight to four, Barty boy."

"Simpson, switch. I'll take him," says Felipe. "You guard Meg."

"Whaddya mean? I'll guard him."

"Bull crap, he's killin' you," says Felipe. "Now switch."

"Uh-oh, ladies," says Mr. O'Connor, "I think the gentlemen are losing their composure."

"I'm takin' him," says Felipe, tossing the ball to Megan.

Felipe comes up tight on Mr. O'Connor, and all six foot three of Simpson is draped over Megan at five five. He just takes the ball away from her, heads toward an easy lay-up, and I can see in his eyes he's gonna dunk it. As he goes up, Mr.

O'Connor comes outta nowhere again and puts the ball back in his face.

"Foul!" cries Simpson.

Big groan from the kids.

It was a clean block and everyone knew it, but Mr. O'Connor doesn't say anything. He just smiles, picks up the ball, and hands it back to Simpson.

"He was all over me," Simpson says, trying to justify his call to everyone else. "Hey, he fouled me."

"No one's arguin', Bart," says Mr. O'Connor, with a sweet, innocent smile. "Come on. Play ball."

Simpson tries to pass in to Josh, but Mr. O'Connor slaps the ball and has it in his hands before Simpson can take a step toward the loose ball.

"No foul, Bart?" says Mr. O'Connor.

Simpson doesn't answer.

Two dribbles and *swish* from five feet beyond the three-point line.

"Nine-four," says Mr. O'Connor.

Katie passes in to Mr. O'Connor. Felipe's right on him. This time, Mr. O'Connor fakes left, drives right, down the middle of the lane. Josh steps in to take the charge, but Mr. O'Connor cuts left with a neat behind-the-back dribble and goes right around him. He starts to go up, as Simpson comes off the weak side to try to block the shot. But Mr. O'Connor goes up over top of him and jams the ball into the hoop.

"Ten-four, fellows."

Next inbound, Katie passes to Mr. O'Connor standin' outside the arc at the top of the key. Fakes right, this time he drives left down the middle of lane, drawing Josh and Simpson toward him. Then a bounce pass back to Katie at the foul line. *Swish.* Game.

Huge cheer from the kids.

"Game, Simpson," says Mr. O'Connor. "Seems to me, guys, you got some work to do if you want to be a real championship team."

He tosses the ball to Felipe and looks right into his eyes. Felipe doesn't say a word, but I think he gets the point.

CHAPTER FIVE

So FOR A FEW MINUTES, MY LIFE wasn't so bad. I was just one of the kids watchin' a great game. My God, was Mr. O'Connor good! I never saw anybody do what he did. How could someone that short stuff it down the throat of a guy who was four inches taller than him and had more than fifty pounds on him?

"Lucky," was all Simpson said.

"Whaddya talkin' about? He ate you up," said Felipe.

"Pick up your jockstrap, Simp," added Josh. "It's out on the court."

Mr. O'Connor was gone a few minutes later, and I went back to shootin'. I shoulda kept my eye on Simpson, but I was lost again in my make-believe world. I shoulda known he wouldn't forget me. I never saw the ball comin'. I went up in the air for a lay-up. I don't jump that high, but when you're off your feet, lots of bad things can happen. This time Simpson didn't miss. Course he was only about ten feet away, but I didn't see him. Just as I jumped and released the ball, Simpson nailed me with the basketball. It took my feet right out from under me, and I crashed to the floor, landing on my right arm.

Now, just because my arm is withered up, it doesn't mean I got no nerves in it. In fact, because there isn't much muscle on it, sometimes it's like it's just raw nerves, at least in some spots. I can't quite move it out from my body to help stop my fall, and I can't get my left arm around in time, either. I just crumple to the ground, with all my weight on my right arm.

So there I am wriggling around on the gym floor like a worm dug up from the ground, and I'm cryin' now, I admit it. I am cryin', 'cause this pain shoots through my arm into my shoulder down into the bottom of my stomach and up into the very top of my head.

"Direct hit!" yells Simpson, as he laughs. "Bull's-eye on a buzza rat."

And I hear kids laughin' at me.

Now I can tell you, you never been alone in life until you're lyin' in the middle of a gym with kids laughin' at you and starin' at you, and not one of them will come over to ask you if you're all right. Not one of them will come over to help you. Not one. And somehow, you have to bite back the pain and swallow down the tears, pick yourself up and walk off that court and out the gym door, past blurred faces of kids whose names you once knew, but now don't. And it's not that you hate them, you just don't ever want to see any of them again. And the one thing you know, you're absolutely sure of, is that you will never go back to whatever you had before this happened. Never.

"He did what?"

For a moment I thought my dad's phone conversation was about me and what Simpson did to me. But I knew better. Nobody in that gym would call my dad about that. What did they care?

"I hope he knows what he's doing," he was saying. "This is going to be very tricky. All right, thanks. I appreciate your calling."

My dad hangs up and looks at Mom and shakes his head. "That was Laura Pollard. She said Mr. O'Connor played a basketball game with some of the guys this afternoon."

"What's wrong with that?" asks Mom.

"Well, nothing, except that I guess he beat them pretty badly. She said he was taunting Simpson. It's just not a good way to start." Then he turns to me.

"Were you there, Jeremy?"

"Yeah," I say. "He was unbelievable, Dad. You shoulda seen him."

"I hope he knows what he's doing." Dad shakes his head again and picks up a newspaper. "Look at this. Even the New York City papers are writing about us. 'Still Waiting,' says the headline. 'Even as convicted rapist'—well, he wasn't convicted of rape, it was attempted rape, but then, they're not much concerned with getting things right—'Gerard Stennard was hauled from the courthouse in hand-cuffs, basketball fans in the sleepy village of Sparrowburg wondered who the new coach would be. Located just one hundred miles north of the basketball capital of the world, affluent Sparrowburg, home to long-range city commuters, seemed poised to make a run at a Class D state title this year. Then the David versus Goliath dream of this the third smallest school in New York State burst when fifteen-year-old Jeremy Chandler walked unannounced into the coach's office to find Stennard molesting a cheerleader.'"

"I was fourteen when it happened," I say.

"As I said, they don't much care about facts," says Dad. Then he looks at me.

"Did this game have anything to do with your being in the gym?"

I'm stunned.

"No."

"You're sure?"

"Why would it have anything to do with me?"

"Why would it have anything to do with Jeremy?" Mom repeats.

"I don't know. Just asking. This whole thing is such a mess."

Did the game have something to do with me? I don't think so, but I do know that Simpson took it out on me, so maybe it did. And what did Dad mean when he said that this wasn't a good way for Mr. O'Connor to start?

CHAPTER SIX

THE SCHOOL BOARD HAD KEPT the announcement of the new coach a secret. Maybe some of the teachers knew, but if they did, they weren't sayin'. Obviously, my dad knew, but he didn't let on, either. Normally, they would have made the announcement at a board meeting, but like all the other times when any question about Coach Stennard came up, they met in private, so the press wouldn't know. The reporters kept hounding Dad for information, telling him that he was legally obligated to tell them what was going on, but he refused to say anything. I think some of them were going to try to take him and the board to court, but then came the day when they were going to announce who the new coach would be, so they dropped their case.

The board decided to make the announcement after school in the gym and make it open to the public.

So here I am at 2:35 P.M. standing by one of the doors, trying to blend in, as my dad gets ready to tell parents, teachers, students, and reporters who the new coach is, because the old coach is on his way to jail, and his son is the guy who is sending the old coach to jail.

My dad and all the board members are sitting up on the stage. Mr. Graves, the principal; Mrs. Pollard, the cheerleading coach; a couple of other teachers, who I think are union reps; and Mr. O'Connor. And now it's starting to add up to me.

Mr. Graves starts to speak. "It is not going to be easy to put what has happened behind us," he says, "but somehow we have to try—for the good of the team, the school, and the community. I know a lot of you are angry with us because we've kept things secret. We thought it was best to do it that way. When the new elections roll around, we'll find out if you agree with how we've handled it." He pauses, thinking maybe they might laugh, but they don't. "Anyway, we spent a lot of time and effort to try to find you a coach who could step into a difficult situation and pick up the pieces and start over. I would be a liar if I told you that everybody isn't expecting this team to win a lot of games, but I will add that getting this school back on track is more important to me than winning games. We tried to find a coach who understands that winning isn't everything, and that healing is more important. With that in mind, I'm going to let Dr. Chandler, our board president, introduce your new coach to you."

Scattered applause.

Here was the father of the kid who ratted on their coach introducing the new coach. I was watching the basketball team. They all sat over on the first row of the bleachers. When my dad got introduced, it was like Mr. Graves had stuck each of them with a red-hot needle in the base of their spines, they couldn't help but jerk upright. Then Felipe looked to the ground. Josh started to fidget. Niko and Leduane looked at each other. Ryley's and Greg's eyes bugged out. Jordan coughed. Paul came out of the dreamland he's usually in, and Simpson almost got up and left.

"I'm not going to dwell on the past," said my dad. "What's done is done. We have to look ahead to the future."

Somehow his words hurt me as much as me getting nailed by Simpson in the gym yesterday. *Not gonna dwell on the past.* Maybe not for him, but I was stuck in the past. I mean, if I could undo that past, I would, because my whole life changed in the past. I couldn't help but dwell on the past. *What's done is done.* It's done all right! My life is done. Done. Done. Done. Overdone, well-done, done forever, done for good, just done!

But then I see Cass, standin' in the doorway across the floor. She wasn't cryin', but close to it. She was biting her lip, and I think she was tryin' to blend in with the wall as much as I was. It hit me a little that this has got to be really hard for her, too. All these months since last March when this whole thing happened, she kept to herself. She was always popular, 'cause she's so beautiful and nice and smart, but I don't see her walkin' down the halls with anyone since that happened. Now she's always by herself. I don't think it's that no one wants to be her friend. I think it's more that she doesn't want to be around anyone else. I know she spends a lot of time in gymnastics and dance, which she always did, but she didn't even go out for cheerleading this year, and she was the captain. In my world, I guess I like things always to be the same. Cass not bein' a cheerleader—well, I guess I never saw a world without her bein' a cheerleader. I mean, obviously, that had a lot to do with what happened with Coach Stennard, but he was gone, and it wasn't her fault, anyway. But I guess it has something to do with the guys, too. I always saw them as my friends, but it was weird, when all this happened, it was like they all grouped together—

against me. And against Cass, too. Not many of them said anything to me except, of course, Simpson. And I suppose he was sayin' things to Cass, too. But I wasn't around him that much to know that. But I'm sure he was. I guess, in the end, I just never really thought about what Cass was thinkin' about and feelin'.

I didn't hear much more of what my father said, until the very end.

"So it gives me great pleasure to introduce the new coach of the Bearcats, Mr. Patrick O'Connor."

Patrick O'Connor. Like I said, it was startin' to add up when I saw him on the stage: the basketball game, his gettin' on Simpson, my dad's comments. So he's the new coach.

Except for a few school board members, a couple of teachers, my father, and Mrs. Pollard, no one's clapping, certainly not the basketball team, although Josh starts to, because he's kind of polite, and he doesn't exactly know what to do. But a quick look from his best friend, Felipe, stops that. In seconds the clapping putters out like a car running out of gas, and now there's only the electric whizzing of the gym lights hanging overhead, as Mr. O'Connor steps up to the microphone on stage.

"Thank you, thank you. Your enthusiasm has touched me," says Mr. O'Connor, sarcastically.

I look at the faces of the kids and the grownups.

This wasn't how they expected Mr. O'Connor to start.

"I want to thank the school board for this opportunity." Then Mr. O'Connor looks hard at each kid on that team before he speaks again. "In one regard," he says slowly, "I disagree some with Dr. Chandler and Mr. Graves—" he looks at them, and adds "—with all due respect. Yes, we have to move ahead. But I don't ever, *ever* want you to forget what happened in the past and what happened to your coach. What he did was wrong. It's plain and simple. He violated a trust. He deserves to be in jail, and anyone one of you," he says looking directly at the guys, "who thinks for a moment that he got a raw deal doesn't deserve to belong on my team."

This was definitely not the way the board had hoped things would go when they introduced the new coach.

CHAPTER SEVEN

THE MEETING DIDN'T LAST MUCH LONGER. One thing that was different was that Mr. O'Connor made a big deal out of introducing Mrs. Pollard, the cheerleading coach, and sayin' that the two of them were going to be working together, because the cheerleaders were part of the basketball team. That was different. I don't know what it means, but I guess I'll find out. Mr. O'Connor told the guys to get ready for practice. Mr. Graves told everyone to leave. The reporters interviewed anyone they could find, and I made sure they couldn't find me. But I was curious to see how practice was going to go, so I didn't leave.

Cass didn't stay much longer. The funny thing with her is that, except for some meetings with our lawyers, we really didn't speak to each other much.

We weren't *great* friends before all this happened, but we were friends. We hung around some. But after—it was weird; she didn't much talk to me. But then, she didn't much talk to anybody.

By now the guys are shootin', and Mr. O'Connor gets done talkin' to the last reporter. He looks at me tryin' to fade into the doorway, but also tryin' to have him see me at the same time. 'Cause I can't stand the fact that this season is finally about to begin, and I'm not gonna be part of it.

Then he starts walkin' across the floor toward me.

"Surprised?" he says as he comes to me.

"A little, but when I saw you on stage, I figured it out."

"Well, obviously, I couldn't say anything to anyone."

"Some of the things my dad had said got me curious."

"Well, listen, Jeremy, like I said, I couldn't say anything to you or anyone until this all got announced. But, uh, well, I'll come right to the point. How'd you like to be our manager again?"

I don't say anything, because I can't believe he said this.

"Well, whaddya think?"

Finally, I mumble, "What about the guys?"

"Whatta bout them?"

"Well, do you think they'd want me?"

"Doesn't matter what they think. I'm the coach."

"Yeah, but—"

"Listen, Jeremy, get it out of your head that you did anything wrong. I'm not naive or stupid. I know what those guys think—about you, about me, about Cass, and about Coach Stennard. They're wrong. It's as simple as that. You did the right thing, the heroic thing."

"I don't feel much like a hero."

"That's why it's heroic."

I stare at the ground.

"I'm not gonna beg you, but this team needs a manager, a good one. One who can help me keep stats, who knows basketball, and someone who loves the game. You're the perfect candidate. But like I said, I'm not gonna beg you. If you want it, the job's yours. If not, I'll find someone else."

I keep starin' at the ground. I know his words are right, but I can't stand the fact that I have to make a decision. What didn't seem fair to me was that I had to decide. Couldn't he just say, you *must* be the manager? Then I'd be off the hook.

"Well?"

I found myself nodding yes and mumbling, "Okay."

"Great!" he says, putting his arm around my shoulder. "Let's get started."

Then he pulls out a silver whistle, blows it loud, and yells, "Guys! Over on the bleachers. Let's get going!"

Next thing I know I'm standin' a few feet away from Mr. O'Connor, every once in a while catching icy stares from the guys, mostly Simpson.

"Like I said earlier, I don't ever want you guys to forget. Understand?"

No answer.

"The answer I expect is, 'Yes, Coach!'"

A few mumbles, of "Yes, Coach."

"I said, 'Understand?'"

This time a few more, louder, "Yes, Coach."

"A lot of things are going to be different on this team, but some things will be the same. One difference will be that the cheerleaders won't be just an accessory anymore. Mrs. Pollard and I have some ideas on how to make that happen. Some things won't change. Your manager was Jeremy Chandler. He's still your manager. Understand?"

There was no, "Yes, Coach."

CHAPTER EIGHT

"JEREMY, OPEN UP MY GYM BAG and hand out a black folder to each player."

I moved slowly toward the bag.

"Come on, Jeremy. Let's get going here. We don't have all night. We've got a lot to accomplish. So hurry it up."

I don't look at anybody's face when I hand out the black folders, but I can feel Simpson's eyes burnin' right through me as he snatches the book out of my hands.

"Jeremy, you take a book and sit on the end by Josh."

Sittin' by Josh wasn't too bad. Out of all of them, it was Josh and Felipe who were the easiest to get along with.

"Gentlemen, don't open the books yet. Just lay

them on your laps," says Mr. O'Connor. "In these books rests your future. Not just for this season, not just in basketball, not just in school, but maybe for the rest of your lives. If you will try to follow what is in these books, your lives may be changed forever. Now, sit up straight, both feet on the floor."

Guys fidget some and sit a little straighter.

"Now!" barks Mr. O'Connor. And everyone sits straight up, except Simpson, who moves slowly into an upright position.

"Open the book to your futures."

There, in big, bold capital letters, reads:

WELCOME TO CONCEPT BASKETBALL

"Welcome to Concept Basketball," reads Mr. O'Connor. "A concept is an idea. An idea requires your thought. But in order for a concept to be really yours, for you to truly understand it, for you to own it, you have to do more than think about it. You have to know it, inside and out. You have to feel it in your heart. You have to be able to state it clearly and concisely. It has to become part of who you are. In the few next weeks and months, you are going to be exposed to a new concept. Not just about basketball, but about your lives. Those who embrace this concept will play a lot on this team, and this team will be successful in ways you never dreamed of. Those who do not embrace this new concept will find coming to practice an absolute agony, and they will not play much, if at all, and the tension between this new concept and their old ideas will be so unbearable that they will quit."

This is a strange way to start a practice.

"Turn the page."

On page two, in bold italic letters is:

It means everything; it means nothing.

"In order to be successful on this team, this is the concept you must first accept, then understand, then embrace, and finally practice."

"What you do on this court, what you do in your lives, means everything. You cannot hope to achieve anything if you do not give all of your energy, your passion, your thought, your will to what you are doing. That is what I expect of you. Every second of every minute of every game of every practice. You must give everything you have, knowing full well that you are not capable of doing that, you still must try. Even though you know that you will fail to accomplish such a challenging feat or achieve such a lofty goal, you must still try to accomplish such a feat and achieve such a goal."

What do those words mean, I wonder to myself. *Knowing you're going to fail, you do it anyway? Why?*

"You have no control over the outcome of your efforts. What you do means everything. You must do all you can, because you cannot know anything about yourself until you give yourself completely, but in the end, your efforts mean nothing. That's the hard part."

There's a long pause. Guys are kind of glancing at each other, wondering what all this means, then Niko puts his hand up.

I need to tell you something about Niko. We got two guys on this team who are adopted. Niko is one. Felipe is the other—well, he's kind of adopted.

Niko is Chinese, but his name is Chris Nicephorus. He's being raised by a Greek family. And Felipe is Spanish, from some country in South America. His father isn't his real father, and I think his stepdad has legally adopted him. But I know he doesn't get along with his stepdad.

I'm not too close to Niko; he's a nice guy, but he's really intense. Really competitive. He's not the easiest guy to warm up to. But he's also a guy who's serious about things. He tries to figure them out. So it's not too strange that he should raise his hand. But I'm not so sure Mr. O'Connor wants anyone to raise their hands right now. He looks over at Niko and nods in his direction.

"Yes?"

"Well, Coach," and the word *coach* slips out of Niko's mouth smooth like a jumper draining the bottom of a net, "if what you say is true, then why bother?"

There's another long a pause, then Mr. O'Connor smiles.

"You're at the first stage of the concept. You're thinking about it."

Chapter Nine

THAT WAS NOT THE ANSWER Niko was looking for. He puts his hand down slowly and looks at his teammates, kinda saying silently, *And your point is what?*

Coach keeps smiling. "In game five of the 1999 playoffs, the New York Knicks, after just barely making it into the playoffs, were playing their hated rival the Miami Heat. The Knicks were an eighth seed; the Heat were seeded number one. As time ran out in game five, Allan Houston took a running one-handed shot. If it went in, the Knicks won; if it missed, the Heat won. The ball hit the rim, bounced up, hit the backboard, and then miraculously came down through the net. The Knicks won and went on to become the first eighth-seeded team ever in NBA history to make it all the way to the championship series.

"In the NBA 2000 championship series between the Indiana Pacers and Los Angeles Lakers, Reggie Miller, one of the best, most consistent three-point shooters ever in the game, took a three-point shot as time expired. If the shot went in, the Pacers won; if not, L.A. would take the lead in the series. Miller, technically a better shooter than Houston, missed the shot. The Pacers lost the game, and though they fought back, they lost the championship in six games. If Miller's shot had gone in, maybe the Pacers would have won the championship.

"Who played harder in their games, Houston or Miller?"

No one says anything.

Finally, Josh says, "They both played hard."

"Exactly. Did Houston *will* his shot to go in harder than Miller did?"

Josh shrugs his shoulders. "Can't say."

"Exactly. Both played hard. Both gave everything they had. Both played like it meant everything. But in the end, they really couldn't control the outcome. And while they may feel good about winning or bad about losing, it doesn't amount to a hill of beans. It's just a game. Okay, turn the page."

THE TWELVE PRINCIPLES OF CONCEPT BASKETBALL

FIRST PRINCIPLE: *Honesty is the First Principle of everything.*

SECOND PRINCIPLE: *Teamwork doesn't work without rigorous honesty.*

THIRD PRINCIPLE: *Teamwork means ego reduction at depth.*

FOURTH PRINCIPLE: *There are no ties in basketball. Never play like the* *best you hope to accomplish is a tie, because that's a lie.*

FIFTH PRINCIPLE: *If you play as if you're trying not to lose, you will.*

SIXTH PRINCIPLE: *You win by either scoring more points than your opponent or not letting your opponent score more points than you. That's the truth.*

SEVENTH PRINCIPLE: *It takes skill to score more points than your opponent.*

EIGHTH PRINCIPLE: *It takes courage to stop your opponent from scoring more points than you.*

NINTH PRINCIPLE: *Skills can be taught.*

TENTH PRINCIPLE: *Either you have courage or you don't.*

ELEVENTH PRINCIPLE: *Great teams are teachable and courageous.*

TWELFTH PRINCIPLE: *My actions will reveal what my principles are.*

"Memorize these principles by tomorrow's practice," said Mr. O'Connor. There was no answer. "Your reply is, 'Yes, Coach.' "

"Yes, Coach," we said, but we weren't all together and we certainly weren't convinced.

CHAPTER TEN

PATRICK SEAN O'CONNOR. Five foot, eleven inches tall. One hundred fifty-five pounds. Guard/forward. *He played forward?* I think to myself, as I read the blurb on him that I found on the Internet.

> Science major; St. Thomas College. NAIA player of the year, junior year. Led his team to an upset victory over Division I powerhouse, Georgetown, scoring thirty-four points, grabbing twelve rebounds, four blocked shots, and seven assists. Led St. Thomas to a second place finish in the NAIA national tournament, scored forty-one points, had seventeen rebounds, six blocked shots, and five assists. Despite his great accomplishments on the court, O'Connor left behind a controversial legacy at St. Thomas. He opted not to play his senior year and was quoted as saying, "I'm not going to let a bunch of half-assed, wannabe basketball players and a half-baked coach ruin my chances at getting into the NBA.

"Jeremy!"

My mom's voice tore into my mind, but I couldn't stop the next thought from coming, *Could this be the same person? What happened to him?*

"Jeremy!" she hollered again. "Time to eat."

"I'll be right down." I wrote down the spot where I found the stuff on Coach O'Connor and then hustled downstairs.

Now all of a sudden it occurred to me that I hadn't said anything to my parents about being asked to be manager. I just always was manager, so I figured they figured I would still be manager, which, of course, is pretty strange to think, since, I mean, I wasn't technically manager anymore. Anyway, there we are sitting at dinner, and it hits me that I have to bring this up somehow.

"What did you think of our announcement, Jeremy? Catch you by surprise?"

"A little, but once I saw him up on the stage, I figured he was the new coach."

"Really? How come?"

"Oh, a couple of things you said, and the way he played the other day. It all added up. Besides, there wasn't anybody else up there who could have been coach."

"Well, that's true. I know he knows the game real well, but I wished he would have been a little less confrontational today."

"I think he's gonna be great," I say, almost in defense of him. "He's got a lot of new ideas."

My parents look at me, and I know I'm standin' at the edge of a cliff about to fall over.

"I hung around for practice today," I say, as I balance on the edge of just enough truth.

Dad sets his fork and knife on the side of the plate, Mom tries to blend into the chair she's sitting on.

"Mr. O'Connor asked me to be manager," I blurt out.

"What?"

"He asked me to be the manager," I repeat.

"What did you say?"

"I said yes."

"Well, you might at least have said, 'I have to talk to my parents about it.' "

"Well, he put me on the spot. I had to make a decision."

"I can't believe he did that, and that you said yes," says Dad, trying to control his temper.

"What's the big deal? I've always been manager."

"Oh, come on, Jeremy, don't play dumb. It would have been better if you let this all blow over for a while. Why did you say yes?"

"I like abuse, Dad," I say sarcastically.

"What?" he yells.

"I like kids making fun of me," I say, almost in tears now.

"What are you talking about?"

The tears are coming out full force now, 'cause I'm so mad that my dad is worrying about the dumb school and what people will say and that he could care less about me.

"I didn't ask to be manager," I say.

"You mean to tell me that you didn't *suggest* to him that you wanted to be manager again?"

I shake my head no.

"Well, we'll see if you're going to stay manager."

Up until the point that Coach O'Connor had asked me to be the manager, I had no hope that I would be. I thought about it, mostly about the way it used to be, but I figured I would never be a part of the team again. But once it happened and I was back as part of the team, and I had this neat new playbook with lots of different ideas in it, well, after that I felt like I *was* on the team again. Even if the guys didn't think I was, or ever wanted me on it. At least Coach did, and maybe Josh did, too. Maybe even Felipe.

So now here was my father saying that I wasn't going to be manager. What was I suppose to think about all this, anyway?

"I wanna be manager," I whisper.

"What did you say?" My dad's voice is threatening now.

"I said, 'I want to be manager.'"

My dad stares at me for a moment.

"Jeremy, if only it were that simple. They're going to think that I maneuvered to get you back on the team as the manager. It's just better if you're not in the spotlight anymore. I think this is a mistake. I'll call Mr. O'Connor tomorrow and tell him that you can't be the manager."

We both look at Mom, trying to figure out which one of us she sides with. She gives us a noncommittal look, like, *I wish this never happened.*

I turn back to my father.

"You know," I blurt out. "I didn't think I'd be manager this year, or ever again. But now, I have the chance to be manager, but now I *can't* be manager." I can feel the power of my anger itching on the inside of my face, tryin' to break free into the air. "You call him! You tell him! Tell him anything you want! Tell him Rat doesn't want to be manager. Lie to him! Tell him anything! I don't care anymore. Not about him, not about the team, not about basketball, not about anything, and I sure as hell don't care about you!" I scream, and then I'm out the door, running down the street.

"Jeremy, get back here!" I hear him yell, but his voice is like the tail of a comet, trailing into a whisper of thin light in the black of night.

CHAPTER ELEVEN

WHEN YOU'RE RUNNIN' HARD AT NIGHT, away from something you don't want to know about or think about, you don't plan where you're goin', you're just goin'. But soon enough you slow down, 'cause you're out of breath, and then you trot, and then walk. And then you look around and see where you are.

I was on the sidewalk, maybe half a mile from my house, and I knew the sidewalk and the street-lights would end sometime soon, and then I'd just be on the side of the road with cars comin' by. Now anybody who's run out of the house like I did knows you have two problems: The first one is, where do you go? And the second one is just as important, how do you get back? I mean, back in the house without having to face the thing you ran from. So what you do is, you just walk, thinking about the problems, and figuring that somehow there will be a solution, even if you didn't know how to get it.

Oh, yeah, I forgot. There's a third problem in November. Right. How long can you stay outside without a jacket on?

And then you start lookin' around, and the bushes on your right seem to be more alive than when you walked by them thousands of times during the day. And then you remember stories about old Harry Howard, the crazy guy who lived in the shack just on the other side of the cemetery, which you now have to walk by. You remember how you once threw a rock through one of his dirty windows on a dare. Somethin' inside me didn't seem right when I threw that rock, but then he came outside with a butcher knife in his hand and swore he'd get the kid with the bad arm, ending any thought I had about wanting to go back and apologize. Besides, nobody ever really talked to old Harry Howard. And, anyway, nine months ago he killed himself, so it doesn't matter anymore. He's buried up in the cemetery. So what's to worry about? I mean, he's dead. He can't do anything now that he's dead. Or maybe he can. I mean if he's dead, well, then he's a ghost, and a ghost can pretty much go wherever a ghost wants to. So you keep walking, and thinking, and maybe now talkin' to yourself, because, well, if you're talkin' to yourself, that will keep your mind off the ghost of Harry Howard, the old crazy guy who killed himself.

Then a car comes by, and now you realize you've got other things to think about, like who was in the car that just drove by. Was it a bunch of guys you know from school? And if it was, well, they'd just love a chance to get Rat all alone, with no father to protect him. Worse yet, in fact, worst of all, it could be Simpson. Yeah, Simpson would just love to get you. And he'd be out at night, too.

Now from up the road come some more headlights. Do you jump off the side of the road into woods where you know the ghost of Harry Howard the crazy guy is, or do you keep walking? Do you wave for a ride or stop and do nothing? Well, only a coward or a crazy guy jumps into the woods, and what do I have to be afraid of? Just keep walking. Pretend this is an everyday thing, which it could be, and is for some people. Course, not for me, but for some people. The car's comin' fast. Won't see me anyway. Just keep walking. Headlights are right on top of me now, and I swear the car's slowing down. Keep walking.

The car definitely slows down as it goes by. Now it's stopping. Turning around. Keep walking. No, run! Jump into the woods. No one will get you! Keep walking. The car is right behind me now. I hear the whir of an electric window dropping down.

"Jeremy, is that you?"

CHAPTER TWELVE

"JEREMY?" COMES THE VOICE AGAIN.

"Cass?"

"What are you doin'?"

"Walkin'," I say, as I step closer to the car.

"I can see that, but it's eight o'clock at night, and it's starting to rain. What are you doin' out here?"

"It's a long story," I mumble.

"Well, get in. We'll take you home."

I open the car door and then think, *It's Josh's car. Cass is with Josh. I wonder if anyone knows that Josh is going out with Cass?*

Josh kind of mumbles, "Hiya, Rat." But I can tell he is embarrassed by the fact that I see him with Cass. Now, Cass is beautiful, with her long straight black hair and deep brown eyes, so it's not like a bunch of guys wouldn't like to be with her, even though she is Puerto Rican, and she's the only Puerto Rican in about six towns around here. But it's not because she's Puerto Rican that there's a problem. It's because of what happened with Coach. I mean, Coach Stennard, that is. Not Coach O'Connor. Isn't that strange. I call them both "Coach," but really, only Coach O'Connor is Coach. I mean, Coach Stennard is headed to jail. And you can't be coach if you're in jail.

Like I said before, Cass and me never really talked about what happened. Not even with the lawyers or the police. Me and her never really talked to each other. And our families aren't like friends or anything. So this is pretty strange. Bein' in the car with her and Josh and all.

"You wanna go home, Rat?" asks Josh.

"S'pose so."

"Why were you out here walking, anyway?" asks Cass.

"Well," I start to answer, but I can't speak too well, because my tongue's heavy and sticky, and my eyes are watering up.

"What's the matter, Jeremy?" asks Cass.

"It's my dad," I blurt out. "He doesn't want me to be the basketball manager."

Cass doesn't say anything and neither does Josh. I wait a little longer, but still they don't say anything.

"S'pose it doesn't matter. I mean, who cares anyway. You guys don't want me on the team, so why should I want to be manager?"

Still, no one says anything.

"It doesn't matter," I whisper to myself.

"Here's your house," mutters Josh.

I get out of the car on Josh's side, saying thanks as I slide off the seat into the rain. As I walk away, Josh says to me, "Hey man, don't say anything to anybody about this, okay? I mean, you know, don't rat me out on this."

I stare at him and blink a couple of times, not quite figuring out what was going on.

"You know, don't go tellin' people about Cass and me. It's not the right time. You swear?"

I nod in agreement, not even sure what I was agreeing to. "No, I won't say anything," I say, and then I head toward the house.

Here I am spillin' my secrets to Josh and Cass, and all they're worried about is being found out. You know, nobody really does care about what's goin' on with me, and that's the truth.

And now I walk back into the mess I ran away from. What the hell, it can't get any worse. Course, when I see my dad and mom sitting in the living room with no television on, just waiting for me, I figure it's about to get a lot worse.

"We need to talk," Dad says, as soon as I walk in.

I sit down on the couch across from him.

"Jeremy, never run away. Whatever it is that you have to face, never run away from it. You understand?"

"Yes, sir," I answer.

"The problems will never get solved if you run away," my mom chimes in.

"Yes, ma'am."

"I called Coach O'Connor," my dad begins.

Here comes the boom, I think. Well, it doesn't matter, anyway.

"Apparently, you were telling me the truth. Coach O'Connor said you had no knowledge that he was going to ask you to be the manager, and that he did put you on the spot."

I can't help but get an I-told-you-so look on my face. But that's understandable, right?

"Well, I'm sorry, Jeremy," my dad says, and then adds, "but having you back as the manager of the team isn't going to be easy for anyone."

Why is it when adults want kids to apologize, they can tell if the kids aren't being sincere? I admit that. Adults can do that to kids. But then, why is it when adults apologize, they skip right over the "I'm sorry" to some explanation of how it's really okay for them to make a mistake? They say "I'm sorry" so fast that a kid never really gets a chance to take it in and enjoy it. A kid never gets time to taste it. Or if you do taste it, it's like choco-late cake followed by a big gulp of sour milk.

"I understand, Dad," I say, letting him off the hook. But I'll tell you, I really don't understand. I mean, shouldn't I come first, ahead of the school and the community, at least sometimes?

"Coach O'Connor really does want you to be the manager," adds Mom.

Apparently Dad couldn't bring himself to say that. If he did, he really would be admitting that he was wrong. And why should they be surprised that Coach really wants me? Do they think that I'm just some mascot with a withered arm? Don't they know that I really do *know* basketball?

"You can be manager, Jeremy," says Dad, "but you have to promise to keep out of trouble with that team. Understand?"

I nod my head, yes, thinking, *I wonder, Daaad, if you could pass that agreement on to Simpson.*

So I head to bed, still manager of the basketball team. With a secret about one of the players and the most unpopular, once-popular girl in the history of the high schools of the world. And with information about the new coach that is really hard to figure out.

"I'm not going to let a bunch of half-assed, wannabe basketball players and a half-baked coach ruin my chances at getting into the NBA," I read again before I shut down the computer.

CHAPTER THIRTEEN

"It's the circuit," says Coach O'Connor. "Each practice, after stretching out, we begin with the circuit. It's nine minutes of nonstop movement. There's nine of you, and there's nine stages on the circuit. One minute at each stage. Stage one: step-ups on the bleachers. Stage two: jumping rope. Stage three: pushups. Stage four: backboard taps. Stage five: pull-ups. Stage six: lay-ups. Stage seven: jump-ups on the bleachers. Stage eight: sit-ups. Stage nine: slide stepping and passes from me.

"After forty-five seconds, I'll blow the whistle and you will race—not jog, not trot, not run—but race to one of the two foul lines, pick up a ball and shoot a foul shot, then chase the ball down and put in a lay-up with your opposite hand. You will yell out whether or not you hit your foul shot and lay-up,

71

and Jeremy will keep track of your misses. Every missed foul shot will net you a sprint at the end of practice. Every missed lay-up, two sprints. You will have only fifteen seconds for all of you to complete the foul shot and lay-up before the whistle blows. If you do not attempt a foul shot or lay-up, they are misses and you run at the end of practice.

"You'll all get a chance at every station, so don't worry about where you start. Oh, and one last point about the circuit: we keep going until everyone finishes each station."

Up until this last statement, I think I understood what Coach was talking about. But what did he mean by saying "we keep going until everyone finishes"?

The guys lined up in front of each station, and the first real practice under Coach O'Connor was about to begin.

Phrreeeett! A short blast and the guys were at the stations.

"Felipe!" yells Coach.

"Coach?" answers Felipe, as he did his step-ups on the bleachers.

"What's the First Principle?"

"Coach?"

"What's the First Principle?"

Felipe stops his step-ups and looks at Coach.

"I didn't say, 'Stop,' did I?"

"No, sir," answers Felipe.

"Get goin'!"

Felipe got going.

"What's the First Principle, Felipe?"

"Don't know, Coach!"

"Give me a sprint right now! Touch the floor at the base lines, foul lines, and half court line. Let's go!"

Off Felipe goes. *Phrreeet* goes the whistle. "Foul shots!" yells Coach O'Connor.

"Got it, Rat!" yells Ryley, and I mark a foul shot for Ryley on the sheet.

"Missed the lay-up," yells Niko.

"Missed both," yells Josh.

Phreeeet! goes the whistle.

"Missed the foul shot," yells Paul.

"Didn't get a chance to shoot!" yells Simpson.

Bang! Bang! On the bleachers. *Slap! Slap!* The rope on the floor.

"Second Principle, Ryley?" yells Coach.

At some point during this practice it does occur to me that all this talk about principles doesn't quite go with what I read about Patrick Sean O'Connor and his college days. Somethin' musta happened along the way to change him.

"Teamwork doesn't work without rigorous honesty!" Ryley yells back.

"Good!"

"Third Principle, Josh!"

73

"Don't know, Coach!"

"Sprint!"

Phreeeeet! "Foul shots!"

"Jordan, Fourth Principle?"

"Can't remember, Coach!"

"Start sprinting!"

"Simpson, Fourth Principle!"

"Don't know!"

"Sprint!"

And so it went. Nine minutes came and went. Then ten minutes. Then eleven. Then twelve. Then—

"Chandler!"

"Yes, Coach?"

"Eighth Principle!"

"Coach?"

"What's the Eighth Principle?"

"Guess I don't know, Coach."

"Run."

And so I ran. For half an hour we ran and tried to complete the circuit. Only Ryley made it to the end, because he knew all the principles.

Phreeeeet!

"Okay, on the bleachers!"

My sweat-soaked shirt stuck to me like syrup on a pancake, but I had to run just like everyone else on the team. Just like everyone else.

"Get your playbooks."

CHAPTER FOURTEEN

NOT EVERYONE HAS HIS PLAYBOOK, which doesn't please Coach at all, and his warning is clear: Don't forget them again, or the entire team suffers.

"The first offense," Coach reads from the book, "is the fast break. The lay-up is still more efficient than the three-point shot. If you took fifty three-point shots in a game and hit fifty percent, which would be a high percentage, you'd score seventy-five points. If you took fifty lay-ups in a game and hit eighty percent, which would be a low percentage, you'd score eighty points, and win the game. Also, the lay-up is more apt to put the other team in foul trouble. So our first offense is the fast-break lay-up.

"The second offense is the guard penetrating as far as he can. The guard drives to the basket for a lay-up, a foul, or if he's stopped, he dishes off.

"The third offense is the two-man game coming off the high post. Where's the high post, Greg?"

"Coach?"

"Where's the high post? Show me."

Greg looks around at the other guys and slowly gets to his feet.

"Show me! That means today!"

Greg hustles to the left of the foul line.

"Good. We can set this up on the right or the left or in the center. It's a very simple play. The guard passes in to the post man, who passes back to the guard, who is swinging to the side and is open for a short jumper. If it's done quickly the guard will be open. If the defense double-teams the shooting guard, the post man can swing the ball to the opposite guard, spin for a jumper at the foul line, or take the ball to the hoop himself."

"Coach?" It's Niko again.

"Yes?"

"We didn't have many plays, so this is all new to us."

"We didn't need many, Coach," adds Greg.

"You didn't?" answers Coach.

"Well, we did all right with only a couple of plays," says Greg, a little quietly.

"You did?" asks Coach sarcastically.

No answer.

"I watched the video of the game you lost in the

first round of the sectional playoffs last year. You lost by eleven points to a team that you had beaten by seventeen during the regular season. They out-played you, they out-hustled you, and they out-thought you. You were the better team athletically, but they wanted it more and they remained disciplined, while you fell apart. Besides, you will note that these are not set plays. This is Concept Basketball: the concept here is movement, always movement, nonstop movement. Okay, let me show you how this works in real life."

"Felipe, handle the ball. Niko, guard him. I'll play high post, and Simpson, guard me. Felipe, let's do this slow at first. You dribble the ball up court and bounce pass to me at the high post. Cut to your right and I give the ball back to you for a short jump shot. Now if Niko stays with you, and either I can't get the ball to you or you can't get a good shot, then I can turn and take a short jump shot at the foul line. Or I can take the ball to the basket for a lay-up. Now, it helps if I can go to the basket with my left, because after we do the simple give-and-go with Felipe, my defender will start to cheat on defense, and he'll try to step out and help on that short jump shot. Once he does that, then I have an open lane to the basket."

We practiced that two-man game over and over again. Coach showed us how to play the pick and roll off the same movement, and even though the defenders knew it was coming, it was almost impossible to stop.

"Again!" Coach yells at Niko and Felipe.

Niko was right up on Felipe. His eyes straining to watch for the pass into the high post. He was up on his toes, ready to slide sideways with every step that Felipe made. His hands moving like an out of control windmill, trying to stop the pass to Ryley at the high post. And then Felipe makes a quick step to the right and Niko goes with him. But Felipe dribbles sharply behind his back and streaks to his left, down the open lane for an easy lay-up. It's a move Coach did not teach us.

Coach smiles and nods his head.

"On the bench, everybody."

We all sit down, happy for a break.

"Open your playbooks to the last page. Some of you may not have gotten this far, but apparently Felipe did."

On the last page in big bold letters:

WHEN ALL ELSE FAILS: HAVE COURAGE!
TAKE A RISK! BE CREATIVE!

"Nice job, Felipe," says Coach. "We're done for the day."

Everyone slowly gets up to head for the locker room.

"Forgetting something?" says Coach O'Connor. "Sprints for the missed fouls shots and lay-ups during the circuit. Thought I forgot, huh? Let's get going."

CHAPTER FIFTEEN

BY THE END OF THE WEEK, the two-man game of basketball that Coach O'Connor had started with had become first a three-man game that got us swinging the ball to the opposite guard, and then a four-man game that included screens away from the ball, reversing the ball direction, and forcing zone defenses to play man-to-man.

"The concept of a zone is very simple and quite simple to break. In a zone, the defender is playing an area. When a player comes into your area, you guard him. In the end, however, all zone defenses have to become man-to-man," Coach explained. "Eventually, the zone defender has to guard *somebody,* not just an area. By finding the creases in the zone, you will force the defender to leave the zone he's covering to play the crease between his area and his teammate's area. Now he's playing man-to-man. Usually two defenders will slide to cover the man in the crease, which means that someone has to be open. If you're the ball handler, your job is to find that open man."

Everyone was learning so much about basketball so fast that it seemed that no one remembered Coach Stennard. Even Simpson seemed to forget. But all that was about to come a quick and painful end.

Just after practice on Friday afternoon, only our fourth day together, Coach O'Connor made an announcement.

"Guys, over on the table at the back of the gym by the locker-room door is a card with a pen next to it. The envelope is addressed to Cassandra Diaz. The cheerleaders were part of this team last year. Cassandra was the captain of the cheerleaders, and she should be the captain this year. But she's chosen not to be. Her decision is at least partly because of you guys. The card on the table is our invitation to have her back on the cheerleading squad so that this team can be complete. Your signatures need to be on that card."

That's all he said. Then he walked into his office.

For a long minute nobody says anything. All the while I'm thinking, *Everything was going along just fine. Why did he do that?*

"The hell with that crap," says Simpson, after

Coach closes the door behind him. "I ain't signin' that card."

Simpson looks around waiting for the other guys to chime in, but no one says anything.

"Are you guys nuts? You're not gonna sign that card, are ya?"

"She never did nothin' against me," says Ryley. "I don't have a problem signin' it."

"I don't care who's on the cheerleading team," says Greg.

"You guys *are* nuts!" says Simpson. "Never did anything against you? She's the one who put Coach in jail and ended us up with this weirdo for a coach."

"Might be weird," says Niko, "but he sure as hell knows basketball."

"You guys are gonna side with him and that spic!" yells Simpson.

"You know," says Felipe slowly. "you're gonna say that word once too often around me, man."

Simpson looks coldly at Felipe, but I can tell he doesn't want to test himself, at least not now. He's a lot bigger than Felipe, but Flip's real muscular, and he has a temper.

"Hey, Flip, it's just that this has got me so pissed off, I don't know what I'm sayin'."

"The hell!" says Felipe. "You know damn well what you're sayin'."

"She's a whore. She's got us all fightin'. Come on.

We're a team. You're not gonna side with that slut, are you? Josh? What about you?"

Now, all through this time, Josh hasn't said anything. I can see his problem. He doesn't want to come out too strong for Cass, 'cause he's afraid the guys might be suspicious, but he's not going to say anything bad about her, either.

"I dunno," says Josh quietly, "maybe it's time to let the past go. Coach Stennard's goin' to jail. He's not comin' back. We got a new coach now. If he wants her to be a cheerleader, I got no problem."

For a minute Simpson doesn't say anything. He just stares at Josh.

"What about you, Rat?" says Simpson suddenly turning on me. "I'll bet this is all your doin'. You want the bitch back, don't you. She's probably doin' you on the side, you little half-armed weasel."

I can see Simpson getting tense, just like Coach Stennard right before he threw the stapler at me, and I can see the looks in the eyes of the other players. They're not gonna help me. Not Felipe—this wasn't his fight, and Felipe only fights for Felipe. Not Ryley, not Greg, not Niko, not Leduane. Not even Josh. I look right at him, and he looks away. Keep his secret with Cass! But don't expect any help. That was Josh, all right. Spineless.

This time, I think to myself, *this time is it.*

Slap! Simpson's open hand catches me full on the

face and I crumple to the ground.

As I lie on the ground waiting for Simpson to kick me, the gym door clangs open, and I hear a cheery voice call out, "Hi guys! Is my husband around?"

No one says anything right away, then Felipe answers softly, "Coach is in the office."

Mrs. O'Connor stops on her the way to the office. "Is anything wrong?" she asks.

"Nothin'." answers Simpson.

"Is that boy all right?" she asks.

"Yeah," says Simpson, pressing his foot up against my back.

"Let it be," says Felipe quietly. "You've done your business. Let him alone."

I stumble to my feet. The side of my face is on fire, and my ear is buzzing like millions of electrified crickets.

"Are you okay?" she asks me.

I nod yes, trying to hold back my tears.

"What happened?" she asks.

No one answers right away, then Simpson says, "He fell."

She looks at me, kind of questioning.

I nod yes again.

"Are you sure you're all right?"

"Yes," I mumble.

"What's going on?" hollers Coach from his office.

So there we all stand, waiting for an explosion.

"What happened?"

"They say he fell and hurt himself," says Mrs. O'Connor.

"That true, Jeremy?"

I nod yes again.

Coach looks around. We're all lookin' down at the floor, not sayin' a word. Finally Coach speaks. "This is my wife, Mrs. O'Connor. Cindy, this is the basketball team. Unfortunately, they haven't yet learned the First Principle—honesty."

CHAPTER SIXTEEN

"THIS PRACTICE IS OVER. JEREMY, I want to see you in my office, now."

I can't believe this is happening, I think to myself as I follow him and his wife like a little boy being sent to his room for lying about eating some forbidden candy before dinner. How many times am I supposed to rat on my friends? Although, when I think of it, Simpson is no friend. And none of them stood up for me, so why should I think they're my friends? They really don't give a damn about me. I'm getting tired of doing this.

It was odd, because this was the first time I had been back in the office since the time with Cass and Coach Stennard. And for a short moment I could see him holding her and glaring at her. Once, on one of those TV nature shows, I saw some hyenas attack a wounded lioness at night. She couldn't defend herself. And those hyenas baited her and bit at her and tortured her all night long, 'til she couldn't defend herself anymore, and she just lay there exhausted. And then they ripped her apart piece by piece, but they didn't do it to eat her. They just did it to kill her. That was Coach Stennard.

Coach O'Connor had moved some things around. His desk wasn't facing the door, it was underneath the window and facing outside, and he had a big photograph of him and his wife and kid hanging on the wall to the left. He's leanin' up against his desk, and his wife is standing to my right, in front of the door. There I am, again, trapped by adults.

"What happened out there?" he says quickly to me.

"I fell," I mumble.

"Honesty, Jeremy, really is the First Principle," he says.

"Coach, please don't ask me. I can't say. I can't do this anymore. I'm tired of telling the truth. It doesn't do any good. I told the truth once, and all it did was cause trouble. I don't have any friends. The guys on the team hate my guts. What good did it do?"

"Do you think you should have lied about what Mr. Stennard did?"

"I don't know what I shoulda done."

"Yes, you do. And you know you did the right thing. It would not have been right for him to get away with what he had done. If you had lied, every time you saw him—or worse, every time you saw Cassandra—you would have hated yourself for not speaking the truth."

"It's easy for you to say, you don't have to live with those guys."

"Actually, I might know more about what you're going through than you think." He looks over at his wife. "I've had to face a lot of the truth about who I am and what I think is important."

I remember the words I read about Coach O'Connor. Maybe he does know something about things like this.

"Someday, if you're interested in being honest, I'll tell you all about how I came to know that the truth really does matter. I'm not going to press you on this incident. I'm pretty sure that Simpson, who probably did not sign the card, is behind this. We'll let it go for now. In a way, it doesn't matter. Unfortunately for you, Simpson and the rest of them are going to think you told me anyway. Even if you say no, Simpson won't believe you. The others might, Josh, particularly, might, but not Simpson."

He was right about that. Simpson wouldn't believe me, and I wonder what he knows about Josh and Cass.

"By the way, Jeremy, another good thing came from your testimony, at least from my point of view—I got this very interesting opportunity to coach you guys. Thanks."

As I start to leave, Mrs. O'Connor speaks to her husband, "You know, Patrick, I could use some help around the house. Megan is up and running around, and I'd like to be able to spend some more time with her and have some more time for my painting. There's still a lot of unpacking to do, and we've got to get the spare room ready."

"We're having another baby, Jeremy," says Coach.

"Oh," I say, 'cause I don't know what else to say. I never quite figured out when it's okay to say things like congratulations, and when it's not.

"I wonder if Jeremy would like to have a job for a few weekends helping us get things pulled together?" asks Mrs. O'Connor.

"A great idea. What do you think, Jeremy? We'd pay you, of course."

The idea catches me off guard, but being around a guy who knows so much about basketball sounds good to me, and making a few dollars wouldn't hurt. Not a lot of people want to hire a one-arm freak. Besides, after the court testimony, it's not like I have a lot of friends to hang with anyway.

"Yeah," I say, "but I'd have to ask my parents."

"Good. If your parents say it's okay, we'll start tomorrow."

CHAPTER SEVENTEEN

"WHY DID HE ASK YOU TO HELP HIM?" Dad was asking me, as he packed some things getting ready for a trip to some conference.

"I don't know, it was kinda his wife's idea," I answer.

"Sounds a little strange to me. I mean, a new coach asking a student for help around the house," says Dad. "What do you think, Diane?"

"It seems fine to me," answers my mother.

"Well, don't you think it's odd?"

"No. I think a young mother who is expecting another child and has a little girl to take care of already could use all the help she can get. Jeremy is responsible and a good worker. No doubt she knows a willing, helping hand when she sees one. I could have used a little more help when I was pregnant."

She had Dad on that one. It's always been a sore point between the two of them. I guess I've heard enough times about how my mother almost lost me before I was born to know that things must have been tough with her when she was pregnant. Dad always gets tightlipped and tense and won't talk about it when the subject comes up.

"Well, I still think it's a strange request coming out of the blue. There must be some reason for it. But if your mother doesn't object—and I can see she doesn't—it's okay with me. But when I get back I think we're going to have to have a long talk about all of this. And don't make a pest of yourself over there."

"Right, Dad," I say, sarcastically. "Thanks."

So on Saturday, Mom drove me over to Coach's house. It was a simple farmhouse out in the country, off on a back road and at the end of a long dirt drive-way hidden between bushes and trees on both sides.

Mrs. O'Connor wasn't too big, but she was gettin' there. Their little daughter, Megan, was about three and a half. She had bouncy curly hair, like little springs stickin' out all over. I wasn't sure just what I was supposed to do at the O'Connors, but pretty soon I was standin' next to Mrs. O'Connor helpin' her fold laundry, which you might not think I can do, but I learned how from my mom, who wasn't goin' to let me go through life pretending that I was helpless.

Megan was sitting up on the dryer trying to help, too, but mostly she was undoing what we had folded. Sasha, their big old golden Lab, was sleeping near the dryer, because it was nice and warm.

And then, kinda out of nowhere, which is how little kids think, Megan asks, "Mommy, how come his arm isn't like his other arm?"

Mrs. O'Connor turns a little red and catches her breath. "Megan, you shouldn't ask questions like that of guests."

But I can see that Megan doesn't understand why she shouldn't ask such questions. Actually, I can't always see why she shouldn't, either.

"Why not?" she asks.

"Well, it's a little hard to explain, but Jeremy is our guest, and we don't just ask questions like that to our guests."

"Why not?"

"Well."

"It's okay, Mrs. O'Connor, I don't mind. It's because—" I say, turning to Megan—"I was born like this. Some people get blue eyes, or brown hair, or—"

"Or curly hair," says Mr. O'Connor, coming in the room and grabbing Megan's hair.

"Yeah, or curly hair. I got one regular arm and one short one."

"Why?" she asks.

I know Megan doesn't want some long, deep answer, so I just say what my mother told me and other kids lots of times, "Because that was God's plan for me."

"Why?" she asks.

"Megan, that's enough questions," says Mrs. O'Connor.

"But why?"

"Because," says Mr. O'Connor, "God has a plan for everyone and a reason for everything He does, even if sometimes we don't always clearly see it. Jeremy may not always know the reason, and neither do we always know the reason."

I have to admit, I never really bought that stuff about God havin' a reason for me havin' half an arm. I sure don't see His reason.

But kinda sudden, I can see Mrs. O'Connor start to tear up and she turns away.

"No, we don't always know the reasons," she says.

Her tears aren't about me.

"I got lunch ready," says Coach.

"I'll tell ya what," I say suddenly to Megan. "I'll bet you I can fold laundry with my one hand faster than you can with two."

"Okay," says Megan.

"After lunch," says Coach.

As we walk into the dining room, I notice a strange painting, some kinda saint, hanging on the wall.

"It's an icon," says Mr. O'Connor to me when he sees me looking at it. "It's called *Madonna and Child.* Cindy painted it."

"It's really—different."

Mrs. O'Connor laughs. "Not so sure you like it, huh?"

"Well, I guess I've never really seen a painting like that."

"The style is from the Russian Orthodox Church," says Mr. O'Connor.

"Oh," I say, "I'm Protestant."

"Well, we're not Orthodox, either," says Mrs. O'Connor, laughing. "We're Roman Catholic, but I've been studying icon painting for many years. I started in college, but then when Pat was playing ball in Europe, I had a chance to study with some masters."

"You played basketball in Europe?"

"Yeah, about five years, mostly in Italy. It was quite an experience. You might say it changed my life," he says, looking at Mrs. O'Connor.

CHAPTER EIGHTEEN

SO THIS IS WHAT I NOW KNOW: Josh is going out with Cass, but doesn't want anyone to know. Coach O'Connor was a star in college, then he badmouthed his teammates and his coach, quit school, and played ball in Europe. I'm helpin' out this same coach, whose wife is pregnant. And, of course, I know that Simpson is still out to get me. Life is too complicated. So mostly I keep my mouth shut and keep an eye out for Simpson.

We covered defenses all that week, and once again, Coach O'Connor had a few surprises.

"If we're playing good defense, we'll be scoring one-third to half our points off turnovers," says Coach. "We'll always start out with man-to-man defense."

"Coach?" says Ryley, putting up his hand.

"Yes?"

"Will this be full-court press? We used to play full-court and a two-three zone."

"No, not strictly speaking," says Coach O'Connor. "Guarding man-to-man all over the court has its pluses, but after a while teams know what you're going to do and a good team can beat it. Same is true for the two-three zone. Having two out front and three underneath the hoop is very predictable. Here's what we'll do. And if you had read your play-books carefully, you would know this.

"When you're on offense," he continues, "the point guard will call out either a color or a number. The color and the number refer to the defense you'll set up after you score. Red, or one, means full-court, man-to-man. Black, or two, means full-court zone trap, but with our big man pressuring the ball on the inbound pass. Orange, or three, means a three-quarter-court zone trap, with no pressure on the inbound passer. Green, or four, means you'll set up in a half-court zone trap.

"Whatever the guard calls, you run, but only if you score. If you don't score, you play man-to-man. If the other teams beat the press, you play man-to-man. You call a different defense each time. Because you're running a motion offense, the other team thinks you're calling an offensive play. So they try to figure what the play is, which, of course, they can't, since you're not calling an offensive play. And, since you're always changing the defense, they never know what you're going to throw at them, or how it is that you know what defense to run. It keeps them off balance and constantly confused. So, you not only out-hustle them, but you outthink them."

"Keeps *them* confused," whispers Josh, "what about us?"

Coach O'Connor's plan was absolutely brilliant, but it did require the guys to think. Which most of them could do—except, Simpson, who, like I said before, was dumber than a moose looking for a mate.

"Okay, guys, I have a little surprise for you. Saturday we're going down to New Brunswick, New Jersey, for a scrimmage. A friend of mine coaches there, so we'll see what we've got."

The looks on the faces of those guys told the whole story: a city school in New Jersey?

"Well, well, well," says Coach O'Connor, looking at them. "I see the idea of testing yourselves against an unknown isn't what you had in mind."

"We never played a school like that, Coach," says Niko.

"That's the point. If you're going to be state champs, you're going to play a lot of schools you've never played before."

This was the first time that anyone had said

what many people had thought—state champs. Was it really possible? Were we that good? If Coach said it, then he must have thought it might be possible.

Everyone started to smile, even Simpson. State champs.

"We'll see," says Coach. "Okay, run your sprints. Jeremy, I need you in my office."

As I walk to the office I hear Simpson snarl, "Once a rat, always a rat." He wasn't ever gonna let that die.

"Jeremy, close the door,"says Coach. "Tell me, have you spoken at all to Cass?"

"Whaddya mean?"

"Well, since you testified in court about Coach Stennard, have you and she spoken?"

"Not really," I say.

"You know, life hasn't been easy for her."

I nod yes, 'cause I know it hasn't. I heard that she's been getting notes in her locker, probably from Simpson.

"That's why I had the guys sign the card to invite her back on the cheerleading team. She needs to be back on this team. Not only for the team, and not only because I understand she's a great gymnast and dancer and the cheerleaders need her, but also to help her put this behind her."

Again I nod yes.

"Well, Mrs. Pollard and I are going to take a ride to her house tonight to give her this card and talk with her and her parents. We'd like you to come along."

"Why, Coach?"

"Because you're part of what happened."

"But I didn't do anything wrong."

"I know you didn't, but you're still part of all of this," he says.

This time I don't nod yes, 'cause even though I know I am part of it, I don't think I want to show up at Cass's house and talk with her and her parents.

"I already spoke to your mother about this, and she's agreed to let you come with us."

Now I know there's no way out, because when Mom's involved it's a done deal.

"What about Dad?"

"Well, I guess your father's away at a conference," says Coach.

Oh boy, I think to myself. *Dad's away; Mom's made a decision that I think he's not gonna like, 'cause he did say to me not to cause any problems, and this one looks like a problem in the making, and I'm caught in the middle.*

I don't need to nod yes; I've been nodded for already.

Chapter Nineteen

"Nice house," whispers Coach O'Connor, as he and I and Mrs. Pollard walk toward the front door.

It was a nice house, too. Kinda formal. With four pillars out front. We walk in through a big red door and I'm face to face with Cass and her father and mother.

"Hi," says Cass.

"Come on in," says her mother.

"Hello," grunts her father, who waves us into the living room with a swing of his head.

So there we sit, three of us on one side of the living room, and three of them on the other side.

"Can I get you something to drink?" says her mother.

"Sure, Coke would be fine," says Coach.

"I'll take the same," says Mrs. Pollard.

I nod my head yes.

"Jeremy, we could use some help," says Cass, getting up to help her mother, and it sure seems strange to me that she would ask me to help, but I get up to go to the kitchen.

Cass stops in the hallway and turns to me.

"Don't say a word about Josh, okay? They don't know anything about that, understand?"

"Sure, don't worry."

"Thanks."

You know, this is the first time she ever said thanks to me. Now I know the thanks wasn't about what happened with Coach Stennard and all. It was about Josh, which is strange, because Josh didn't even stick up for her with Simpson. And he didn't stick up for me, either.

So there we sit, sippin' sodas in Cass's living room, waiting for someone to break the ice.

"Well, let's get to the point," Cass's father finally says.

"Well, Mr. Diaz," says Coach. "I've got a card here from the basketball team for Cass. They would like her to be back on the cheerleading squad."

"They would, would they," he says, almost shouting.

"And I have a card from the cheerleaders, as well," says Mrs. Pollard. "It's just not the same without Cass. The girls really need her. The school needs her."

"Really," says Cass's father sarcastically. "You're lucky Cassandra is even going to your school. It's only because there isn't another school near here and because she pleaded with us to go back there. I should never have moved here in the first place. "

"Dad—" says Cass, but he cuts her off.

"I don't want to hear anymore of this. She does nothing wrong and this *gentuzo* tries to hurt her, and somehow she's to blame. These *gringos* make fun of her. They tease her. They even threaten her. And now you want her back to be a cheerleader. No."

Mrs. Diaz starts to say something, but he turns to her and talks to her in Spanish. Then Cass says something to him in Spanish.

"Don't argue with me," he says to her.

"I'm not trying to argue, I just want you to listen to me for a change. All my life I've done what you wanted. I get good grades. Almost always in the nineties. I've never been in trouble. I've never made you ashamed of me. Then this happens."

Cass pauses, like saying "this" brings the whole memory of "this" into the open; like saying "this" lets everyone in the room into that disgusting moment of what the word "this" really means. She closes her eyes and gulps back her tears. "I did nothing wrong. Nothing!"

Her mother reaches over to hug her, but Cass pushes her away.

"No! I need to say this. You need to hear it. All of you. I did not do anything to lead him on. He was the one." Cass closes her eyes, shakes her head a little, like she's arguing with herself about just how much of "this" she's going to tell us. Then she looks right at me. "Jeremy is the only one who knows what really happened, and he didn't see it all. But he knows enough to know the truth."

Everyone turns to me. All I can do is shrug my shoulders and nod my head a little.

But they keep staring at me, waiting for me to say again what I said in court. Finally, I mumble, "Cass didn't do anything wrong. It was all Coach Stennard. He was wrong, not Cass."

Cass smiles at me. "*Gracias,*" she says to me. Then she turns to her father. "Dad, I like the girls on the cheerleading squad. They're my friends. Right now, some of them are the only friends I have in that school. I didn't do anything wrong. You said that yourself, but you treat me like I did. You treat me like I was the one who did something bad."

"I never said that," he argues.

"You should listen to your daughter," says his wife. "You do treat her that way. Watching her every move. You treat her like she's disgraced you and this family. It is you who should be ashamed."

He says something back to her in Spanish.

I don't know what it is he said, but, boy, she didn't like it.

"*Mi Padre, te amo,*" says Cass. "But you have to let me live my life. The only way to show the *gringos* is for me to be who I am. I am a Puerto Rican girl. I will always be a Puerto Rican girl. Always to them—and always to me."

He says something else to her in Spanish, then he smiles, and turns to us. "Okay, Cassandra wins. She always does, you know."

He picks up the card from the basketball team, and then looks at Coach. "This is your idea, no?"

Coach nods yes.

"Mr. Diaz, I have to tell you that not everyone signed it."

Silence.

I can see Cass kinda roll her eyes like, *Why the hell did you have to say that.*

Mr. Diaz looks intently at Coach. "You are an honest man."

"You would have found out sooner or later," says Coach.

"That's true. And the ones who did not sign it—what are their names?"

"You know I can't tell you that, but you'll find out—"

There's only one, I think to myself.

"Sooner or later," says Mr. Diaz.

Coach smiles a little.

Mr. Diaz nods his head. "But you, as an honest man, can you give me your word that those who did not sign this card will not hurt Cassandra?"

Coach pauses and nods yes. "I give you my word."

I wonder just how he expects to keep that promise.

CHAPTER TWENTY

"CHEERLEADERS SIT IN THE BACK, basketball players up front," Coach was sayin' as we boarded the bus for New Brunswick. "Here's the seating arrangement."

"What?" Greg was asking. Greg was asking that because he had been going out with one of the cheerleaders for about year, and this was time for Greg and her to—well, whatever—it wasn't gonna happen this time.

Actually, I kinda wanted to sit near Katie Callahan. At a small school like ours, the girls could play basketball and be on the cheerleading squad. Katie did both. Our girls' team is good, but I guess they would have gotten killed by this big school, so the girls were only going as cheerleaders.

"Front seat, Felipe and Simpson," Coach says.

Felipe and Simpson, I think to myself. *Well, that's one thing he can do to keep Simpson away from Cass. No trouble on the bus, anyway.*

The girls didn't have pre-assigned seats, a point more than one of the guys on the team tried to make with Coach. "They're not trying to win a championship," is all he would say.

It was unusual for the girls to be going on this trip, too, since it was only a scrimmage, but Mrs. Pollard and Coach had arranged for the cheerleaders to meet with the cheerleaders down at this school to see some new cheers and stuff.

Mostly I slept and stared out the window as we drove.

New Brunswick looked scary to me, just because it was a city. The school was big. Huge. The biggest school I've ever seen. The gym looked like it could seat thousands.

When we walked in, the other team was already practicing. I think there was only one white guy on the team. But then there was only one black guy on our team.

The coach from the other team was a tall black man.

"Pat, how are you? It's good to see you," he says, giving Coach a hug.

His team has stopped shooting and are watching him now.

He blows his whistle and they all run over to the

bleachers. They hustle a lot faster than our guys do. I have a feeling this is going to be a long scrimmage for our guys.

"Guys, this is Coach Patrick Sean O'Connor. He and I played ball together in Italy. He's one of the best shooting guards I've ever met, and if you're not paying attention on the court, one of his passes could take your head off. I know. I can still feel the pain on the side of my head."

"Thanks, Ray," says Coach. "I guess you guys already know about your coach's work ethic," Coach says to the guys on the bench, who groan out a yes. Then he turns to our guys, "Okay, boys, the lockers are over there. Get changed quickly and get warmed up. Let's see what you've learned so far."

So Coach played ball in Italy with this guy Ray. Another piece to the puzzle.

Like I figured, these guys were really good. They put on a clinic. It was sixteen to nothin' before we scored a point, and that came because Felipe beat their guard when he tried to steal the ball but missed. Felipe got free for a moment and hit a long three-pointer. They played a three-quarter court zone press that we couldn't figure out. We played four ten-minute quarters, which they dominated, and then took a break, but Coach didn't seem to get too upset. About the only thing really great that happened was the time Felipe beat his man by going left on him, taking the ball around his back, and then spinning in the air for a left-handed lay-up. Coach called a time out.

"What was that?" he asks Felipe.

Felipe smiles at him and says, "Last page of the playbook, Coach," which brings a smile to Coach's face, too.

"Right, Felipe, 'When all else fails: Have courage! Take a risk! Be creative!'"

After we played the four quarters, Coach had our guys work with the other team. Mostly they worked on how to do that three-quarter-court trapping press, and how to beat it. Every once in a while the cheerleaders would come in, I think to check out our guys. Not much else happened that day, except for two things.

One happened when I went out into the hall to get a drink of water, and I overheard some of their cheerleaders talking with Cass.

"You're a Puerto Rican, girl. Whaddya doin' hangin' with all them?"

"That's who lives near me. It's not like we hang. Where I live, there aren't many Puerto Ricans," Cass laughs. "I'm it."

"Not quite," says another girl. "There's one guy there who's Latino."

"You mean Felipe?"

"Whatever. All I know is he's *guapo*."

"Well, he's not Puerto Rican," says Cass. "He's from South America or somethin'."

"Well, all I know is you're Puerto Rican, and that boy, whatever he is, is *mui guapo*."

Cass doesn't say anything, and then one of the girls sees me and says something in Spanish, which they laugh at, even Cass. Like always, I figure someone said something about my arm, which happens all the time. But it is hard to have Cass laugh, too.

"Just wanted some water," I mutter at them. But inside, well, inside I hurt like I hurt on the outside when Simpson knocked me down with the ball. My God! Why did Cass have to laugh, too?

The other thing happened right at the end of the scrimmage, when the guys were heading to the locker room. Coach O'Connor was talking with the coach of the other team and one of his players. I was getting our stuff packed up.

"Jeremy," hollered Coach. "Come here for a second, would ya? I want you to meet somebody."

"This is James Hunt," says Coach O'Connor.

I nod, "Hello," and so does he.

"This is the guy I told you about, James," says the other coach.

James looks at me and nods his head again.

"Coach told me you testified against your coach," he says.

I kinda look at Coach O'Connor, who doesn't say

anything or do anything. I look back at James and nod my head yes.

"In court?"

Again, I nod yes.

"I had to do that once, too. 'Bout my aunt. I was ten. It ain't easy. Everybody told me I was doin' the right thing. Didn't feel like it. I was scared. Really scared. That guy kept starin' at me. You scared?"

I shrug my shoulders a little, because, I don't know if I was scared or not. I just didn't want the guys on the team to hate me, but I don't think I was scared.

"Yeah, I was scared. But that guy's in jail now, and he ain't gonna do to anyone else what he did to my aunt."

Then James reaches over and shakes my left hand in that cool way I've seen black guys shake hands.

"Thanks, James," says his coach.

I was still thinkin' about that when I was walking out of the door to the bus. Ten years old, testifying in court. I guess I didn't see the actual testifying part as a big deal. What I couldn't get past was the fact that the guys on the team saw me as different after I testified. I didn't see me as different.

I was already in my seat when Cass got on the bus. She didn't look at me, in fact, she didn't really look at anyone, including Josh, who was definitely looking at her. And Simpson was looking at her, too. And I could see that Simpson could see that Josh was staring at Cass. Simpson's not real bright, but I know he was figuring out that something was going on between them.

CHAPTER TWENTY-ONE

DAD DROVE ME OVER TO COACH'S house on Sunday.

"So what do you do for Mrs. O'Connor?" he says as we're driving down the long dirt road to the house.

"I dunno. Fold laundry, play with Megan."

"You enjoy it?"

"Yeah."

That's about as far as our conversations usually go. There's not much else to talk about. My life and his life are so different. I don't really know much about him being a doctor. When I was younger, I used to care, or, at least, I thought I cared. Anyway, they have pictures of me when I used to dress up and pretend I was a doctor, so I guess I cared. But then I started to play basketball, and he never really cared about that. I can do lots of things, even though

I got a bad arm, but sometimes I feel like Dad doesn't think I'm quite complete. That, somehow, because of my arm, I'm gonna be some kinda freak or invalid all my life.

Coach was outside when we drove up.

"Dr. Chandler, good to see you," says Coach.

"Mr. O'Connor, good to see you. Jeremy said your guys had a real lesson in basketball yesterday."

"Well, yeah, they did. But it was what I expected. Ray Dunbar is an old friend of mine from when we used to play ball in Italy. He's a great coach. His guys are always well-disciplined, as well as talented. I wanted the boys to see what it takes to be a champion. Come on in for a cup of coffee?"

Now, most of the time Dad is too busy for coffee with someone, but for some reason he says yes. Maybe because he's curious about Coach. So in they march.

"By the way, most people around here call me 'Doc.' "

"Well, most people I know call me Pat," says Coach.

Megan peeks out the door and I hear her squeal to her mother, "Jer'my, Jer'my's here."

"Jeremy has been a big help around here," says Mrs. O'Connor to my dad, as Megan pulls her toward me. "Megan just loves him."

I can see a strange look on Dad's face when Megan reaches up to hold my hand. It's like he didn't expect me to be a big help to anyone, and he didn't expect some little girl to really be attached to me.

"That's great," he says, but I can tell he's embarrassed about all the attention on me. It's weird: I mean, what did he think was going to happen to me? Because I got a bad arm I was just somehow going to stop growing up? Or because I got a bad arm, I can't think and do things and be useful and friends with people? Or maybe it was just that he didn't realize that I was growing up?

Megan pulls me into the laundry room to show me all the clothes she folded by herself. Dad's in the kitchen next to the laundry room talking with Coach and his wife.

"Actually, Dr. Chandler," says Mrs. O'Connor, "we've been meaning to get in touch with you. Obviously, I'm pregnant. We've got an obstetrician we're working with at the hospital, Dr. Yu."

"He's very good," says Dad.

"Yes, he is," says Mrs. O'Connor. "But, being out here in the country, and in the middle of winter, we thought we'd like to stay in touch with you, just in case things get complicated.

"We've got a four-wheel-drive car," adds Mr. O'Connor.

"Sure. I'll give you my pager number. I am going to be out of town for a few days, but if you need me, of course, I'll help."

"Thanks," says Mrs. O'Connor. Then they look at one another.

"There is one other thing you need to know," says Mr. O'Connor quietly. "Cindy has cancer."

There's a long silence. *Cancer,* I think, *that's like saying you're gonna die!* I know my dad has had patients who had cancer, and most of them are dead. My God, she's got cancer and she's gonna have a baby.

"The doctors discovered it right after I learned I was expecting."

Long silence.

"We're both Catholics," says Mrs. O'Connor. "We don't believe in abortion."

Another long silence. I think to myself, *I wonder why they said that?* Now, I can't see them, so I don't know what they're doin', or what kind of look my dad might have given them. Suddenly, I think, I wonder if Dad ever did an abortion?

"I'll call Dr. Yu tomorrow," says Dad, matter-of-factly.

CHAPTER TWENTY-TWO

BOOM BOOM BOOM BOOOOOOMMMMM! Boom Boom Boom Booooooommmm!

The sounds of a symphony call me over to Coach's office before practice starts, and I listen at the door.

"We're going to start with this—Beethoven's Fifth. The cheerleaders have a dance routine set to it, believe it or not. Now I need you to—"

My curiosity gets to me and I have to knock.

"Come in," hollers Coach.

I open the door and there sits Coach, Mrs. Pollard, and one of the seniors, a kid we call Snore, because his name is Zachary Zeller, which got shortened to Z. Z., which, of course, got changed to "Snore."

"Jeremy, you know Zachary," says Mrs. Pollard.

"Hey, Snore," I say.

"Yo, Rat," he says.

Snore is one of the few people in the school, maybe in the whole county, who can call me Rat and not have it mean anything to do with Coach Stennard. Snore could care less about basketball. He probably doesn't even know Coach Stennard is gone or in jail. All he cares about is music. I can't figure out why he's sittin' here with Coach and Mrs. Pollard, but I soon find out.

"We're going over the music and lights for the halftime show," says Coach.

I guess Coach was serious about having the cheer-leaders really be part of the team, I think to myself.

"Zachary here is going to provide the sound system and lights."

"It'll be good. Very good," whispers Snore. "Yes, indeed, very good."

"You're sure you can do this?" asks Mrs. Pollard.

"Oh yeah, oh yeah. No problem. I can do this fine. I'll listen to the B-man; I've always liked him, you know, very ahead of his time. I put the lights in the four corners and some others around the gym and match them to the booms of the B-man. It'll be great!"

Mrs. Pollard gives Coach one of those, *Are you sure he can pull this off?* looks.

"What the heck," she says. "Wait'll you see the new outfits for the cheerleaders. Nobody else in the county will have anything like it."

"Okay, first home game tomorrow night!" says Coach.

There couldn't have been a better script to an opening night. The gym was packed. Snore did just what he said he would. The lights pulsated to the booms of Beethoven, and the cheerleaders, dressed in brand-new, one-piece, loose-flowing pantsuits of crimson red and black stripes danced to a number that Cass had choreographed.

The motion offense that Coach had designed had the other team bumpin' into each other or just standin' flat-footed as our guys went right by them. The other team couldn't figure out what the colors and numbers the guards were yelling out meant. We won by forty-four points, and Coach wasn't even tryin' to run up the score.

It was a perfect night—until the very end, that is.

"*EEEiiiiiiyyyeeee!* That bastard!" It was Cass screaming. I could hear her all the way from the boys' locker room where everyone was getting dressed. All the guys look up in surprise. All except Simpson. He was smiling.

Niko noticed Simpson first.

"This your doin'?" he asks Simpson.

"Don't know anything about it," Simpson says with a shrug.

"I'll bet," says Niko.

"Why don't you leave her alone?" asks Ryley.

"Whaddya talkin' about?" Simpson replies.

"Whatever it is, it's got your trademark all over it," says Greg.

"Couldn't be me. I was playin' ball all night with you guys." Simpson smiles.

"That's what I mean—a Simpson trademark," says Greg. "No fingerprints."

"What did you do this time?" asks Ryley.

"First of all, *I* didn't do anything. But *if* I did do something, which, of course, I didn't do . . ."

"Of course," mimics Niko.

"Then what I might have done is leave some calling cards just to let her know how much I enjoy seeing her back on the cheerleading squad."

"Calling cards?" asks Greg.

All this time, I'm watchin' Josh and Felipe; neither one is sayin' anything. They're just watchin' Simpson.

"Callin' cards," says Simpson. "Let's just leave it at that."

"Whadidya do, Simpson?" Josh blurts out suddenly.

"Whoa, Joshua!" Simpson says. "What do you care?"

Chapter Twenty-Two

"What callin' cards, Simpson?" says Josh, loudly.

"What I did or didn't do to that bitch is none of your business!"

"I'm makin' it my business, and she's not a bitch," says Josh.

"What? You goin' out with her or somethin'?" says Simpson.

Josh doesn't answer. The silence is all the answer anyone needs.

"Well, I'll be damned," says Simpson smiling. "Joshua's goin' out with the spic!"

"You know," says Felipe slowly, "I've told you before that you were goin' to use that word once too often."

Simpson had gone too far, and this time he wasn't goin' to back down. He looks right at Felipe, his smile fades. "Spic," he says like he was slurpin' a thick milkshake.

Felipe was on him in a flash and crashed Simpson up against the lockers. All the guys jumped in to break them apart, and the next thing I knew Coach and Mrs. Pollard were standing in the locker room.

"Knock it off!" Coach was yelling.

"That's enough! Stop it!" yells Mrs. Pollard.

Ryley and Josh pull Felipe off, but before Niko and Greg could grab Simpson's arms, Simpson nailed Felipe with a shot to the jaw.

"Cheap shot, Simpson. That's what you are," says Josh.

"I don't know what this is about," says Coach, "and your fighting better not be about what we just found out."

Everyone stops, even Simpson, because, well, because the fight *was* about what they just found out, even if we didn't know what it was they had found out.

"Someone humiliated one of our cheerleaders." Coach's voice is getting louder and his face redder. "Someone did something despicable, and I think somebody on this team knows about it and maybe even planned it.

"I told you the First Principle of this team is honesty, but I see I'm talkin' to animals who don't know a damn thing about honesty and principles. You guys are disgusting, because you know who it is and you don't have the balls to say anything about it." And now he's really yellin'. "You antagonize, tease, and harass Jeremy, but he's the only one here who has the guts to tell the truth, no matter what it costs him. And it cost him friendship with the guys he cared most about. But you guys aren't worthy of his friendship. You're worthless pigs! And I'm not going to put up with this slimy behavior. I'll throw you all off the team! I'll play the season with junior varsity kids! I'll forfeit the season! But I'm not going to tolerate the crap that just happened tonight! You understand me?"

"Yes, Coach," a few mumble.

"I can't hear you!" he screams.

"Yes, Coach!" they holler back.

"I want some answers, and I want them now! Who was responsible for degrading one of our cheerleaders?"

Again, silence. Coach starts to say something, but Ryley speaks up.

"Simpson, Coach. I think Simpson did it."

"You lyin' son of a bitch! You got no proof."

"Maybe not, but you been out after her from the start!" answers Ryley.

Coach looks around the room. Everyone of the guys on the team nod yes. Then he looks at Simpson.

"You got some explaining to do."

"Whattaya talkin' about? I don't have to explain anything. Not to you, and not to any of these ass-holes."

"That was your one and only chance. You're through, Simpson. Hand in your uniform," says Coach.

"You can't prove I did anything. It's their word against mine!"

"I don't need to prove anything," says Coach. "This is my team, and you're not on it anymore."

"Kiss my ass! All of you can kiss my ass. You're all a bunch of losers. You're all rats, just like the little weasel with the scrawny arm." Then Simpson looks right at me. "Your old man shoulda made you an abortion when he had the chance."

"Get outta here, now! You're through," says Coach.

"Through? You think I'm through? I'm not through. I'm just beginning," says Simpson, as he picks up his gym bag and heads out the door.

CHAPTER
TWENTY-THREE

I WONDER IF IT HAS TO DO WITH the time of the year? I mean, things always start to go rotten for me when Christmas is comin'. It's supposed to be a season filled with happiness and joy and all, but it never is for me. I wonder why that is? I walk home as a light snow falls like white dust sifting through the one lone streetlight near my house. It should have been a great night. We won, and we won big. But it's like we were back to square one—or at least I am. Simpson's off the team, and he won't be pleasant to be around for me. At least when he was on the team, Coach could kinda keep him in check. Now, I'm all alone.

I walk up on my porch and I can see Dad on the phone. And Simpson's words, which I pretended to myself didn't matter, are sittin' in my brain just as real as my father on the phone. "Your old man shoulda made you an abortion when he had the chance." I know it's stupid, but I can't stop thinkin' about that. Because, somewhere in my thoughts about me, about who I am, what I was, and who I'll be, always was and is this question: *I wonder what my mother and father thought when they saw me for the first time—with my crippled arm. I wonder if Simpson is right. I wonder if my dad ever did think that.* Like I said, I know it's stupid, but it's a funny thing with thoughts like that: You can tell yourself they're stupid, but some part of you keeps sayin', *Yeah, maybe they are stupid, but they might be true.*

"Well, I suppose it was unavoidable," he says, as I walk in. Mom's standin' in the kitchen and looks at him as he hangs up the phone.

"Coach O'Connor had to throw Simpson off the team," he says to her.

"Why?" she asks.

"He did something to Cassandra Diaz. Coach O'Connor had no choice."

"That's too bad," she says. "He's had a hard life."

He's had a hard life, I think to myself. *What about Cass? Hell, what about me?* Then, they both see me standing there.

"You know anything about this, Jeremy?" asks Dad.

126

"Probably as much as you. Simpson did somethin' stupid to Cass. There was a fight with him and Felipe, and Coach threw him off the team. Not much more to it."

Dad shakes his head and sits down.

"I remember the night she died," says Mom. "I think Simpson was about nine or ten."

"Ten," says Dad, kinda to himself.

"She had been fighting the cancer for a long time," says Mom.

I've heard Mom talk about Simpson's mother before. This is a small town and everybody knows everybody. But I guess I never realized that Mom knew Simpson's mother that well.

"We were good friends. She was very smart. In fact, we were going to go away to college together. But, well, we didn't."

"What happened?" I ask.

"Well, she fell in love, and well—"

"What, she got pregnant?" I ask.

"Yes, she got pregnant," Mom repeats.

"Simpson?"

"No," says Mom. "She lost the baby."

I'll bet! I think to myself. An abortion. I look over at Dad. I wonder if he was the one who did it.

"She shoulda lost Simpson," I say.

"What!" says Mom.

"Simpson's an idiot," I say.

"Never say that someone should have lost a baby!" Mom yells at me. "Never! You understand?"

I'm stunned. Mom's never like this.

"Sure," I mumble.

Ssccrreeeeeeech!

"Asshole!" The cry screams through the night snow and echoes through the living room.

"Who was that?" asks Mom.

"Simpson," says Dad.

Like I said, when Simpson was on the team, at least Coach could protect me. Now I was alone. And it hit me, finally, hit me, that I really was alone. Someday, somewhere, Simpson was going to get me, and my *friends* weren't gonna do anything to stop him. There was nothing Mom and Dad could do. They couldn't go to school for me or with me. And there wasn't much Coach was gonna do now; he had done all he could. Simpson was off the team. There was nothing left for Coach to use as a threat to keep Simpson in line.

And when I thought of Simpson, I thought of what he said about my father.

Every once in a while, sometimes in the morning, sometimes at night, sometimes on weekends, I look in the mirror. I mean really look, and ask myself— "Who is this person I'm lookin' at?" I know a lot of kids do this. Nobody talks about it, but a lot of kids do it. And the reason nobody talks about it is that

everyone would think they're weird if they admit-
ted to doin' such a thing. But kids do it.

And another reason why nobody talks about it is
that when you do it, you're all alone, and whatever
answers you get when you ask the question in front
of the mirror only mean something to you.

So when I look into the mirror at myself, starin'
up close at my face, and I ask the question, "Who is
this person?" tryin' to find an answer, eventually,
my eyes drift down to my arm. I can't stop from
doing it. I can't escape the fact that my arm isn't an
arm like everyone else's. I wish it wasn't that way,
because why would Katie Callahan ever think I'm
cute, ever go out with me? Why would any girl ever
go out with a crippled freak like me? Why was I
ever born?

So you can kinda see why what Simpson said
might have been stupid, but there might be some
truth to it.

All night long, just when I would drift off and
lose myself in some television show, my thoughts
would snap back like a light switch that was off and
then suddenly flicked back to *on*. And there would
be Simpson—tomorrow, school, Simpson. And there
would be the questions about me, Dad, my arm.

Then comes the horror of slipping into the cold
sheets of my bed, alone with my thoughts in the
dark. I reach over for Tigger. I used to snuggle with

him when I was younger, and now I pull him close to me again. Wrap both my arms around him and tuck him below my chin. Then I curl up in a ball.

"I don't know if you can hear me," I say, "or if you listen to kids like me, God, but if you do listen, well, then, make all of this go away somehow, because I feel all alone, and I have for a long, long time. I never really complained to you about my arm. You know I wanted a good one so I could play ball and have girls like me. But I never really complained to you about that, because I figured it didn't really matter anyway. I mean, I had a bad arm and that was that. So I've been good about my arm, God. But why is it you're letting Simpson loose on me? What did I do to deserve that? And why do I have to be all alone, anyway, God? That I don't understand. And I wonder, God, since we're talking, why did you have me born? It can't possibly be true, what Simpson said about Dad and making me an abortion. But just tell me, why am I here at all? I know I don't pray like I should, but maybe you could hear me this one time. Cause I gotta tell ya, God, I don't know how I'm gonna get up in the morning and get outta this bed, and get myself to go to school. And I think you know what I mean."

CHAPTER TWENTY-FOUR

I WONDER IF THERE'S SOME special part of the brain that lets you stick things in it that you can't figure out, so that you can forget them and get on with life without having to deal with them. That's what must have happened last night with me. 'Cause I was thinkin' about Simpson, and Dad, and my arm, and then, somehow, I stored it all someplace and then I was asleep. But then it was morning and I woke up.

Of course, the things that got stored woke up, too. Every once in a while, when you're just minding your own business, up these things come, erupting in your stomach like a fiery volcano, filling you with its burning hot lava: *You gotta go to school today, and Simpson will be there waiting. It might not be today that he gets you. Maybe not tomorrow, but someday. And someday you're gonna have to talk to Mom, and someday you're gonna have to talk with Dad, too.*

Somehow, and I do wonder how, I pull down the covers of the bed, slip one leg and then two out of the warm bed, put on my clothes, and go downstairs to a mom who is totally unaware of the fear that's got me.

Mom's washin' the dishes loud and hard, the way she does when she is upset about somethin'. I know it doesn't matter if I keep quiet or talk, she'll eventually just blurt out what's buggin' her. I guess she has that same kinda volcano. Sure enough, I'm in the middle of a big bite of cereal when it erupts.

"I don't like what you said last night," she blurts out.

"Mom?" I mumble through the milky cereal.

"You know what I mean. About losing a baby. I don't know where you got those thoughts."

"I didn't mean anything by it."

"Then you shoudn't have said it."

"Look Mom, it's just Simpson," I say.

"Just Simpson! I don't care who it is. And I told you, his mother was my friend. I don't want you to talk like that."

"Like what, Mom? All I said was—"

"I know what you said, you don't need to repeat it. I just don't want you to say such a thing again."

And now it's my volcano that explodes.

"Do you know what it's been like for me, because of him?" I yell.

Mom looks at me, and I can tell that she hasn't thought about that at all.

"All you care about is Simpson. Why don't you think about me?

"Jeremy—"

"He shouldn't have been born. He shoulda been an abortion!" I yell as I plow out the door.

Somehow explosions push you on to the next event, but explosions don't solve problems. If I make it through the problem of Simpson, I come home to the problem of Mom. Explosions do change other problems, though. Like, right now, I could care less if the guys on the basketball team like me.

What explosions do is to turn you into a robot when it comes to the rest of your life. You go through the day kinda half alive. But when you remember the explosion, you know you're still alive, because that feeling inside of you keeps bubbling up, wanting to explode again.

So the robot part of me knew this: We had won our first game, and easily, too, but now Simpson wasn't on the team, and although he was a pain in the butt, he was a good rebounder. Coach tells the team that what Simpson did was "reprehensible." I had to look it up. It means really terrible, so bad that it can't be overlooked or even forgiven. So what did he do? I never found out exactly, but it seems he filled up Cassandra's locker with condoms, and wrote all kinds of nasty notes. So Coach threw him off the team, and now Coach is telling the guys that we can win without Simpson and . . .

"Even if we don't win, I'm not going to allow a player to disrespect anyone the way Simpson did Cassandra Diaz. Get this through your heads—the cheerleaders are part of this team, too."

It's a nice thought, but no one really believes it.

It was not an easy practice. The guys didn't have much energy at first, but after Coach yelled at them, they started to hustle.

I didn't have to face an explosion back at home. Worse. Nothing. I was ignored by Mom. She did what she always did, but she didn't much talk to me. So went the week.

In school, I kept a watchful eye out for Simpson, who seemed to leave me alone, except for occasional names in the hallway, or bumpin' into me on purpose. I tried a little to talk to Mom about stupid stuff, but mostly we kept out of each other's way.

We won our next two games without Simpson, and then it was the weekend, and Dad had dropped me off at Coach's house. No one answered the door, so I just walked in.

Coach was correcting papers in his office, just off one side of the kitchen.

Chapter Twenty-Four

"Mrs. O'Connor's in her studio. Go ahead in," he says, when he sees me.

I walk to the other side of the kitchen to see Mrs. O'Connor sitting in front of an easel with a large canvas on it. There was a candle burning in the room, and it smelled kinda funny.

"Jeremy," she says, "I didn't hear you come in."

"Just got here."

"Megan's still napping. Come on in. It'll take me a few minutes to clean up," she says, draping a cloth over the painting. "This is a very special one," she says, nodding toward the painting. "It's very unusual for me to try, because I don't have a painting to work from. Usually, I copy icons that have already been painted by great masters. This time, I'm going only by descriptions, and there aren't many for this saint."

She goes over to blow out the candle.

"There's a lot more to painting icons than just painting," she says. "You have to have the right atmosphere. That's why I light the candle and burn incense."

Knock. Knock. Knock.

"I got it, honey," yells Mr. O'Connor, as he walks to the front door.

"Mr. O'Connor?"

"Yes?" says Coach.

"I'm Mr. Theodore. Simpson's father."

Uh-oh! I think to myself.

There's a long pause.

"Can I talk to you?"

"Sure," says Coach. "Come in. Would you like a cup of coffee?"

Mr. Theodore must have said yes, because I can hear Coach getting some cups.

"Milk or sugar?" asks Mr. O'Connor.

"Black is fine," he says. "Is there someplace we can talk?" he asks Coach after he gets his coffee.

"Sure," says Coach, motioning him to his little office.

"Mommy," comes a voice from upstairs.

"Megan's up," says Mrs. O'Connor. "I'll be right back, Jeremy."

So there I am standin' in her art studio that's back-to-back with Coach's office.

"I'll get right to the point, Mr. O'Connor. I know Simpson can be a handful. Nobody knows that better than me. But you can't kick him off the team," Mr. Theodore pleads. "Basketball is all he's got."

"I can't overlook what he did," says Coach.

That's because it was reprehensible, I think.

"There has to be a way, something he can do. You don't understand."

There's a long pause, then Mr. Theodore begins again. "Listen, you have to know. He's had it hard. Simpson's mom died when he was ten years old. It tore him apart. Cancer, slowly. A little each day. He watched her disintegrate into nothing before his eyes. Each day he'd come home, and each day she'd be worse. At first, I could see the hopeful smile on his face. He'd bring things he did in school to show her. Drawings. He got good grades. He's a smart kid. He'd come running into her room, and she'd try to be happy for him, but it was just too much. After a while he wouldn't bring home anything. And soon enough he stopped going into her room. He just quit." I can hear Simpson's dad cryin' some now. "Maybe I did, too."

Another pause.

"Basketball was the only thing we could do together. I wasn't much on knowin' how to talk to anyone, 'specially not my son."

Neither is my father or my mother, I think to myself.

"But we could play basketball together. You can't kick him off the team. Please."

It's funny, you know, I never thought Simpson had a father. I mean, I knew he *had* a father. I've seen him around plenty of times, but I just never thought about what kind of a man his father would be. And until the other night, I never really thought about his mother bein' dead. I knew she had died, but I just never *thought* about it. It's funny the things we don't know about people. It's funny how

137

when you find them out it starts to change how you think about them. Some things I don't think I'd like to know.

"I don't know—" says Coach. "He'd have to make some serious amends."

"He can do that, I know he can."

"He'd have to apologize to the team."

"He can do that."

"To the cheerleaders . . ."

"Okay."

"And specifically to Cassandra and her parents."

Mr. Theodore didn't respond right away.

"To her parents? Why to her parents?"

"Well, because what Simpson did was—"

Then Coach cut himself off.

"You know, I don't think this is going to work."

"Why, what are you talking about?"

"Why didn't Simpson come to see me himself?"

Silence.

"Well, I thought I should come and see you first."

"Why?"

"Well, because, he's not ready yet."

"Does he even know you came over here?"

"What are you talking about?"

"Well, let's just say that it should have been your son here himself talking to me."

"He'll come over."

"When he's ready?"

"Yeah, when he's ready," says Mr. Theodore, and I can tell he's starting to get mad.

"I think it should have been him to begin with," says Coach.

"I told you, he'll come over."

"I'm sorry Mr. Theodore, but this meeting should have been Simpson's idea. He should have initiated this, not you."

More silence.

"You and I both know that you're going to need him on this team."

"Actually, I don't know that."

"You can win this league championship, but you're not going any further."

"I think this conversation has come to an end, Mr. Theodore."

Another long silence.

"I'm sorry, Mr. Theodore, it's best if you leave now."

"Okay. I'll leave," says Mr. Theodore loudly. "You're a fool, O'Connor. A complete jerk. I hope you and that team falls flat on its face."

CHAPTER
TWENTY-FIVE

WELL, WE DIDN'T LOSE, at least not the next three games. So now we were six and zero, which is what people expected anyway. Simpson showed up at all three games, sometimes drunk, I think. He never cheered for or against us. He would just stand there and laugh whenever one of the guys made a mistake. When it looked like we were going to win, he'd leave.

Cass stayed on the cheerleading squad, but I think she stopped seeing Josh. I wasn't sure about that, because they never talked openly about what they were doin' anyway, but I think she was staying to herself even more.

Me and Mom had stayed outta each other's way, but on Saturday, she said she'd drive me to Coach's house, and I knew that this was goin' be the time to revisit the explosion.

Like I said before, it doesn't matter if I'm silent

or I talk, Mom's gonna eventually say what she wants. So I figure, why bother speakin'?

"Jeremy," she begins, and I feel the muscles in my neck tighten. "Do you know why I got so upset about what you said?"

What a dumb question, I think to myself. *Why do mothers ask questions like that? If I knew why, maybe I wouldnta said it. On the other hand, I'da probably still said it, even if I did know why. And, maybe, deep down somewhere, I do know why.*

"No," I say, partly because it's true, and partly because it's what she wants me to say anyway.

"I'll tell you," she says.

You're gonna tell me anyway, I think.

"You almost didn't make it. I almost lost you."

Now, I knew I was premature. They told me that lots of times, but somehow, I was getting more of the story now.

"It was touch-and-go for a while. You were four weeks premature."

"What does that mean—'I almost didn't make it?'" I ask.

"Well," she pauses. "Because you were premature, you weren't with me in the hospital. I would walk down to the nursery room you were in. Watch you through the glass. Talk to you. Pray for you. One day, I went down there, and you weren't moving." I can see the tears startin' to drip down Mom's face.

"You were starting to turn blue. I yelled for the nurse, but no one came. I started screaming, and finally someone got you. They told me later that they had literally pronounced you dead."

There's nowhere to hide in a car. You're just strapped into starin' at whatever is in front of you. But in the moment of lookin' straight ahead, comes great freedom. And in freedom comes the need to know something real about life. My life. This fact of my birth—of my almost death—frees up a question down deep below all the volcanoes that ever spewed in all my years alive.

"Why do I have this arm, Mom?"

She starts to say the usual thing about God's plan, but I'm not a little kid anymore. It might be God's plan, but there's somethin' more to it than that, and I know she knows somethin' that I don't know about all this. Like maybe there was another plan. Another option.

But then we pull into Coach's long driveway, and there's a car sittin' on the road near the driveway. Simpson is sittin' behind the wheel, kinda slumped down, half-hidden below the dashboard.

"Wonder what he's doing there?" Mom asks out loud.

"Don't know," I mumble. *But it ain't good,* I think to myself.

When we get to the house, Coach is out on the porch sweeping some rugs.

Chapter Twenty-Five

"Hello, Mrs. Chandler," he calls. "Like to come in for a cup of coffee?"

"You know, I think I will," Mom answers. "I'd like to see just what Jeremy does for you over here, so that he can do it for me at home."

"You don't pay as much as they do, Mom," I say.

"You're lucky you have a room to sleep in and three meals a day." She laughs. It was a joke, but just as Mom says it, she looks at me.

"I guess I am," I say.

"Cindy's upstairs resting," he says, as we walk into the kitchen.

I can tell by the way he says that and the look on his face that Coach is concerned about his wife. I mean, I suppose he was always concerned, but maybe I just never saw it. Anyhow, I can see that the concern is like, well, it's like, maybe she's not gonna make it. I guess I never thought about that. I mean, I figure everybody makes it. I mean, I've never known anyone who died. Not really.

"She's upstairs, lying down. I'm sure she'd like a visitor. Come on up."

Mrs. O'Connor was on her side, eyes closed, but she opened them right away. Megan was curled up next to her sound asleep.

"Thought you might like a female-type visitor," says Coach, "since you're always stuck with me."

Mrs. O'Connor smiles, as Coach sits on the bed.

So there I stand, watchin' and listen' as my mom talks with Mrs. O'Connor, and you know what I keep thinkin' about? Simpson. That's right—Simpson. Simpson out in the car. Simpson at the games, laughin' at us. Simpson makin' fun of me and hittin' me with the basketball. Simpson and what he's gonna do, 'cause he's gonna do somethin'. And—as weird as it sounds—Simpson with his mother. Simpson standin' in a room like this, starin' at his mother, like this. Watchin' her try to smile at him, with pale pink lips and heavy eyes, like this. Watchin' her die.

CHAPTER TWENTY-SIX

BY THE TIME I WAS BACK at Coach's house on the next Saturday, we were eleven and zero. Snore, Mrs. Pollard, Cass, and Coach had put together some really great dance routines. There was one dance to a weird song called something like "Carmina Burona," by a guy named Orff; maybe that one was Coach's idea. Then there was a really cool one to an old song called "Red Hot Love." Then they did one that had cannons going off, called the *1812 Overture,* and another one called "In the Mood," and another by some group called Cheap Trick.

The area newspapers were all covering our games, and some of the city newspapers had little stories about us, and they were talking about the dances by the cheerleaders, too. So maybe Coach was right about them being part of the team.

Simpson was still showing up at all the games. Coach didn't say anything about him at practice. And when we pulled up on Saturday to Coach's house, Simpson was at the end of the drive again, but there was another car in the driveway by the house.

"Is that Simpson?" asks my mom, as we pull into the long driveway.

"Yeah," I say.

"I wonder why he comes out here," she says, but as soon as she says it, she knows the reason. "Is he out here often?"

"Yeah, ever since he was thrown off the team."

"That's too bad," she says, shaking her head.

Then I shake my head, like I can't believe she just said that. I can't believe that she's back on the 'feel sorry for Simpson' crusade.

"What did you do that for?" she asks.

"What?" I say, pretending like I don't know.

"Don't give me that attitude. Why did you shake your head like that?"

"Why'd you shake yours?" I say.

"Don't talk to me like that!"

I say nothing, but I do shake my head again.

"What is going on with you, young man?"

"Nothin'."

"Maybe we oughta turn right around and go have a talk with your father."

"That'd be great! That would solve a lot of problems," I mutter to myself, sarcastically.

"What?"

"Nothin'."

"What did you say?"

"It doesn't matter."

"It does too matter!"

I don't say anything.

"Answer me!"

"I said, 'It doesn't matter!'"

"Don't you use that tone of voice with me."

"What tone of voice? Okay, Mom, you wanna know what's goin' on? I'll tell you. All you care about is Simpson. It's poor Simpson. He's had it hard. We should think about Simpson. Do you know what that guy has done to me? Do you!"

Mom doesn't answer.

"He's made my life hell, and all you care about is him."

"Jeremy, I—"

"And as far as talkin' with Dad—that sounds like a great idea," I say sarcastically. "Let's talk to Dad, who probably never wanted me born!"

"What are you talking about?"

So now it was out in the open, just like I knew it always would be. Because the brain can't keep those things tucked away forever. Like I said, they drip into the stomach and then explode when you don't expect it. Like you're not even thinkin' about it, and then *splussh,* up it comes and you're covered all over with puke.

"Didn't want you born?" my mother says, kinda whispering.

I nod my head yes.

"Oh, Jeremy, whatever gave you that idea?"

I don't look at her, and I never answer her. I just open the door and stumble up the steps to Coach's house.

"Jeremy! Jeremy!" I hear her cry, but I don't look back, and she doesn't follow, and I slam the door behind me.

"Hello?"

"It's me, Mrs. O'Connor," I say, realizing that I never knocked.

"Oh, Jeremy, it's you. I'm back here in the studio," she says. "Come on in."

As I walk in, I see her covering up the painting she's working on, which is the second time she's done that. She sees me looking at her.

"Special painting," she says, kinda explaining why she's covering it up.

She blows out the candles that are always burning when she's painting and puts away the incense burner.

"You like the smell?" she asks.

148

Chapter Twenty-Six

"It's okay."

"Kinda strong, huh?"

"Yeah."

"It's called frankincense. It reminds me that painting icons is a gift."

"Oh," I say, pretending to understand, but I have no clue what she's talking about.

She can see I don't, so she goes on.

"Frankincense was one of the gifts that the three Wise Men brought to the Christ child. It helps me remember that what I'm doing is giving a gift—my painting is a gift to others—because I was given a gift of having the talent to paint."

I don't know if I understand much more, but she keeps talking about this. Adults will do that—take an idea they have and just keep talking about it until they see you have no idea or interest in what they're saying or until you really do understand what they're saying.

"I've been given many gifts," she says, as she cleans up. "Painting, a great husband, Megan, a new baby," she says, touching her stomach, "great friends, a great life. What about you, Jeremy?"

"Ma'am?" I say.

"What about you? What gifts have you been given?" she asks, as she puts away her paints.

Why would she ask me such a question? I have no idea what gifts I've been given. Pretty much, none. I got a bad arm, no friends, no chance of Katie Callahan ever liking me, a mom I just yelled at, a dad who—I don't know what. Making a list of my gifts isn't high on my list. But Mrs. O'Connor is not letting me off the hook.

"Oh, come on, Jeremy, what gifts do you have?"

You know there was somethin' about Mrs. O'Connor that I couldn't hide from. Maybe it was that she was gonna have a baby and that gave her some kinda power or beauty that I couldn't get away from. She was beautiful. Not just in her shiny reddish-brown hair that curled around her face, or in her green eyes, but deep inside her. Maybe it was the baby. Maybe it was the love that comes from havin' a baby. What hit me when I'm standin' there was that I never once heard her complain or even talk about the fact that she had cancer. It was always about other people—even now, it was about me.

I shake my head a little from side to side. "Haven't really got any gifts," I mumble. "Or, if I do, I don't know what they are."

"Oh, I doubt that's true," she says. Then she stops what she's doing and looks right at me. "Jeremy, maybe you don't know this about yourself, but you have one of the greatest gifts of all—you have a conscience. Telling the truth is important to you."

No one had ever said that to me. But I think it is true. But where did it get me? So why is it important to tell the truth?

"You know, painting icons has a lot to do with telling the truth. You have to learn to paint the all-seeing eyes. The eyes in the face of an icon should follow you no matter where you go, or where you stand to look at the face. The eyes of the icon are the conscience," she says to me with a smile.

"We're back!" hollers Coach, as he comes in the back door with Megan and Sasha, the dog.

I look at Coach, with his little girl, his pregnant wife, who has cancer, and who paints pictures of saints with eyes that follow you and pierce you—and I still can't figure out what happened to him. What changed him from a selfish college player into this guy who loves his family so much and teaches kids about things like honesty?

CHAPTER TWENTY-SEVEN

A CONSCIENCE—THAT'S A GIFT? That's what I'm askin' myself when I walk up the porch after Coach drives me home. Doesn't everybody have a conscience? No, not everybody. Not Simpson, that's for sure. Felipe? If he does, it only goes as far as Felipe. Josh? Does a conscience mean you stick up for your friends? So, Josh doesn't have one. Niko? Ryley? Greg? Any of them?

Cass? Now Cass is hard to figure. I don't know. In this whole swirl of events, she's at the center, but I honestly don't know about Cass. It coulda been somebody else in Coach Stennard's office. Why do I even call him Coach? He's no coach—he's nothin'. He certainly has no conscience. It didn't matter if it was Cass, it coulda been Katie. If it had been her, I'da gone after him. I woulda hit him with the stapler. Why didn't I hit him when it was Cass? Why was I such a coward? Maybe that's what's buggin' me about this whole mess. I really did nothin.' I just stood there like some moron. Mumblin' and stammerin' and sayin' nothin'. Maybe that's the whole problem. Maybe Mrs. O'Connor is wrong—maybe I don't have a conscience. I mean, if you have a conscience, don't you do somethin' when you see a girl about to get raped?

I think I'm tired of growing up. Last year, everything was about perfect. Well, maybe not perfect, but at least things fit in place. This year, nothing fits. Is this what growing up is supposed to be? If it is, well, it sucks!

Dad's sitting in his chair, and I'm hopin' I can get by him, 'cause I'm not up for talkin' to him much today.

"Jeremy," he says in a soft voice as I try to sneak by. "I'd like to talk with you."

You know, when a parent or a teacher says, "I'd like to talk with you," it really means, "I will talk with you, and I will talk with you now." It's not like a kid can say no.

"Sure," I say, tightening my stomach.

"Your mother, well, your mother told me what you said about me. Son, I just don't understand why you would say such a thing."

I had almost completely forgotten about what I had

said in the car to Mom. It seemed like the thing I wanted to say at the time, but right now, I wish I hadn't said it. For one thing, it means talkin' to Dad when I don't want to. For another, I'm not so sure I meant it.

"Why would you say such a thing?"

I'm thinkin' to myself, *To tell you the truth, Dad, I don't even remember what I said, but at the time, it seemed real important.*

"Why in God's name would you possibly think that I didn't want you?"

I shrug my shoulders, like I don't know why I said it.

"Jeremy, this is serious," he says.

"I don't know, Dad. But, well . . ."

"What brought this on? Have you been thinking this—has this been bothering you for a while? What happened?"

The thing of it is that I guess I have been thinking about it for a while, but I can't say that to him.

"Simpson said that you shoulda made me an abortion," I blurt out.

"Simpson! You'd believe something he said?"

"Well, it's not so much that I believe him, it's just—"

"Just what?"

"You musta known you were gettin' a kid with a bad arm. You musta thought about Mom having an abortion, didn't you?"

154

Now here's where the truth is really powerful. I had Dad on that, cause I could see from his look that he had thought about it. And nothin' else he was gonna say could take that thought away, erase it from existence. He had thought about making me an abortion. And he was guilty for that thought. I knew it. He knew it.

"Your mother and I always wanted you. We love you."

He can say what he wants, but we both know that he thought about killin' me because I have a bad arm; because I'm a freak. Now I could let him off the hook here, because deep inside me I know, really know, he does love me. But I don't let him off. He squirms. I say nothing. Then the phone rings.

"Hello," says Dad. "Yes, Pat. What is it? Did you call Dr. Yu? Sure, I can come over. Yes, I'll bring him along."

Dad hangs up the phone. "Jeremy," he says, all business, like the conversation before never happened. "That was Mr. O'Connor. He needs me to come over right away."

Long pause.

"He needs you to come along to watch Megan. Get your things, you may be staying overnight."

That's the amazing thing about my dad. I don't know if it's good or bad, but he can turn off his emotions like turning off a faucet. One quick twist of the wrist and the water stops.

"Come on, Jeremy. We need to go now."

All business. Conversation over. Get in the car. There's a job to do.

It was snowing heavily. Neither one of us speak the whole way to Coach's house, but just before we get out of the car, Dad says, "I really am sorry that you think that I don't love you. I know you may never forgive me for what I thought. But everybody *thinks* things. It's what they do that matters. And I know you may never believe me, but I love you very much, and I always will."

CHAPTER TWENTY-EIGHT

"TOXEMIA. SHE'S GOING TO HAVE TO stay in bed, legs elevated, maybe until the end of the pregnancy. You're due the first week of March, right?"

"I can't stay in bed—" Mrs. O'Connor was struggling to say. "There's too much to do."

"You can stay in bed here at home for the next few weeks and curl up with your daughter," Dad says, nodding his head toward Megan, who was sound asleep next to Mrs. O'Connor, "or you can stay in bed in the hospital without your daughter or your husband. Your choice."

"I'll be a good girl," says Mrs. O'Connor.

"She'll stay in bed here," says Coach. "Dr. Yu will be back day after tomorrow, and we'll be in to see him then."

"Keep her legs up and make sure she stays in

bed." Then he turns to me. "Did you bring your stuff in with you?"

I nod yes.

"Can you use Jeremy's help?" he says to Coach.

"Always."

Dad smiles a little at me, then turns to Coach. "He's a good kid, you know."

"Yeah, he is," says Coach.

Dad looks back at me long and hard, "See you tomorrow, Son."

I don't say a word.

Coach is standin' by the stove, gettin' ready to boil some water for tea. I can see he's lookin' at me as I watch my dad walk out. He starts to talk, kinda to me, but without looking at me.

"Tough day today?"

"Coach?"

"Well, you kinda kept pretty quiet today when you were here earlier, and, well, you don't have to be a rocket scientist to see that you and your dad aren't exactly on good terms, although it does appear that at least he's tryin'. Want some herbal tea? Got one here called Tension Tamer. Probably good for both of us."

"Sure," I mumble.

"Want some honey in it?"

I nod my head yes.

"So," says Coach, handing me a cup of tea and sitting down. "You wanna talk about what's goin' on?"

"No."

"Sure?"

"Yeah, I'm sure."

Then all of sudden a whole bunch of questions about Coach that have been buildin' up inside of me begin to bubble up and I know that if I'm ever gonna ask them then now's the time. Once I start, it's like tappin' a pencil in class. You don't ever tap it just once.

"What happened to you in college? Why'd you say those things about your team and coach? You don't believe them now. What happened in Italy?"

Coach looks at me a long time. I don't know if he's gonna yell or laugh.

"Been waiting a long time to ask, haven't you?"

"Sorry, Coach, but—"

"No, you're not sorry. You gotta know. That's okay.

"I didn't get drafted by the pros, the way I hoped when I finished college. Why I thought I'd get drafted even though I didn't play my senior year is one of the dumber ideas I've had. I knew I was short, still, I had a lot of talent. But I also had a reputation for being a hothead and a troublemaker. I said some stupid things."

"Yeah, I know," I say.

"What, you look me up in some college hoops Web site?"

"Yeah."

"Well, it's public knowledge, no harm done. So, no pro offers from the NBA, but along came a chance to play in Europe. Cindy and I were engaged. We got married and headed for Italy. I thought I was going to be a star over there, but I was greatly mistaken. The players were good, really good. A lot of them played hard because they knew there could be an NBA scout in the stands on any given night. But not everybody played hard. There were some players who didn't have the self-discipline not to get in trouble.

"I wasn't on the starting team right away. For the first time in my entire basketball career, I was sitting on the bench. It was horrible. It didn't take long for me to start badmouthing the coach and other players. Soon enough I was hanging out with guys who didn't care about working hard. A few beers after the game. Staying out later and later. Then one night, someone had some cocaine. I don't even remember who. I had never gotten into the drug scene in college, but I was drunk this night, and I really didn't care about much, so I figured, what the heck. I loved it from the start. It was like for the first time ever, I could erase all that tension from trying to be the best. I think I was addicted to coke from the very beginning, maybe even from before I ever used."

"But you're not addicted now, right? I mean,

you're not usin' cocaine now. What happened?"

"Well, I am still addicted. Once you're addicted, you're always addicted. But I'm a recovering addict, which is another story. But as to what happened . . . well, two things happened. One was Ray—

"The coach from the school we scrimmaged."

"Yeah, Ray Whitfield, Jr. What a guy. Ray was one of the guys who worked hard. He was good enough to make the pros, but he blew out a knee at the end of his junior year in college, and then went to Italy to play himself back into the eyes of the scouts. He was on his way, and then he blew out the knee again. He played a few more years, but everyone knew he would never make it to the NBA. Ray learned to speak Italian, and he worked with kids in the cities. He was devoted to his family and to his religion. Ray was the one who helped turn my life around. He was there when Cindy had trouble with our first child."

"Megan?"

"No, not Meg. His name was John Francis. He didn't make it."

"Oh," I say, but I don't look at Coach, I was afraid he might be gettin' teary-eyed, and there's nothin' worse than bein' alone with an adult when they get weepy. So I remind him: "You said two things."

"That's true. The other thing kind of involved Ray, but it's a long story. Not bad tea, uh?"

"No, it's pretty good," I say.

"So that's my story. What about you?"

"Coach?"

"Whatta bout you? Things not going so good with your dad?"

"Guess you could say so."

"Does a lot of good to just talk about things," says Coach.

"It's no big deal," I say, then I pause, thinkin' 'bout if I'm gonna talk or not, and finally I add, "It's really hard to talk about."

"Sure seems like he loves you."

"Yeah, well, you don't know what I know."

"Probably true. But I just told you about me. So what do you know that I don't?"

Still, I don't look at Coach, but for some reason, words just start to slip out, one after another. "One thing I know is he didn't want me born."

"You know that for a fact?"

"Yeah, I do. He thought about my mom havin' an abortion when he knew I would have a bad arm."

Coach looks at me hard for a long while, then he looks down at his tea.

"Let me tell you about the other thing that happened to me. Like I said, it involved Ray Whitfield. Cindy was pregnant and about to give birth. The night she went to the hospital, I was out partying with some guys. It was Ray who took her to the hospital. It shoulda been me, but I was too stoned. There were some complications with the birth. Actually, there were problems with the pregnancy right from the start, but I was so out of it, I never realized it.

"After Ray took Cindy to the hospital, he came to find me. I was high and drunk in some bar. In walks Ray. I'm smiling and ready to glad-hand him and offer him a drink, even though he doesn't drink. Just as I start to stand up, Ray reaches down, grabs my shirt, and jerks me to my feet. I'll never forget what he said to me. 'Your wife is in the hospital, about to give birth. She may lose your baby, and she may die. You get to your feet now and act like a man! Your family needs you.'

"He took me to his house, threw me in the shower, and his wife, Yvonne, poured coffee in me. Then he marched me into the hospital just in time to see the nurse carrying away my newborn son. Only he wasn't newborn. There he was, a fully formed little person—but he was dead.

"Jeremy, I would have given anything to get that moment back in my life, to have that boy, my son, born alive. Not to have been out drunk while my wife suffered so. But I can't. I think maybe I know how your father feels. I never had a chance to make amends to my son. Your father does and has. You can't hate him forever for a thought he once had."

CHAPTER TWENTY-NINE

"OF COURSE YOU'RE GOING TO CHURCH," Mrs. O'Connor was saying. "I'm fine. The phone is right by my side. You're going to have to leave me alone when you go to work, anyway. So go. Take Megan and Jeremy with you. Church would do you good, Jeremy."

"But I don't have any good clothes," I say.

"Are you kidding?" Coach laughs. "We're Catholics. Catholics don't get dressed up, except for maybe Easter and Christmas."

"That's not true, Pat," says Mrs. O'Connor.

"Is too true. Why, I once showed up with a tie on, and they threw me out of church."

"Pat . . ."

"Yes, Jer'my. You come to church with us," squeals Megan.

"I've never been to a Catholic church before. I won't know what to do."

"Well, there's a lot of kneeling and standing and sitting, but not much singing. So just do what I do," says Coach.

So there we sit in church, me starin' at all the pictures of saints and the big crucifix on the wall that actually shows blood coming out the side of Jesus, which kind of weirds me out, 'cause I never really thought about how Jesus died. The death part is kind of freaky. The part where God sits in someplace called heaven and there's lots of angels and nice people, that's fine. But the part about there once being a man named Jesus who actually lived and died a horrible death; that part I have trouble with. 'Specially, 'cause I think, well, if he was God, like, why didn't everyone know? And why didn't he just say, "*Pooff!* You're all saved and I don't have to die." And how can God die, anyway? I mean, if you think about it, it's all pretty weird stuff.

Church wasn't so bad, except when everyone went up to get Communion, and Coach told me just to sit there. I mean everyone else got the bread, but not me? That's kind of strange, but what do I know?

But as everyone was going up to get the bread, I see Cass and her family. I didn't notice them during the service because I was plunked behind a big white pillar. But I see them get the bread and walk back to their seats. There's Cass, looking very beautiful; her dark black hair falling down around her shoulders. Her head was bowed, looking down at the floor, and walking fast, like everyone else. I strain my head to look around the pole without anyone noticing that I'm trying to see her, and then, there, waiting for her, is Felipe. Felipe in church, waiting for Cass. Maybe those girls down at that big school were right about Cass and Felipe. But like I said, what do I know?

"The mass is ended," says the priest.

"Thanks be to God," says everyone else.

The priest and the kids who light the candles walk out, and everyone else files out right after them. Now the organ's still playin'. The choir is still singin', course nobody else is singin', but the choir is. But people are talkin' to each other, rushin' to get out. It seemed rude to me. I mean, aren't you supposed to be quiet or something at the end of church? Aren't you supposed to be changed because of church? No one looked much changed to me. Or maybe it was just me. I wasn't changed, that was for sure. But then, I didn't get the bread.

And don't you know it, just as we're about to walk out the door, we walk right into Cass and Felipe.

"Hey, Coach," says Felipe.

"Hello, Felipe, and Cassandra. Good to see you."

Chapter Twenty-Nine

"Yeah, well, uh, good to see you," Felipe mumbles.

"Hey, Jeremy," says Cass, "I didn't know you were Catholic."

"Nah, well, no, I'm not, but, well, Coach and Megan," I say, looking down at Megan.

"Jeremy decided to join us this morning to keep Megan company," says Coach.

"That's cool, Rat," says Felipe. And I can tell that he means it, so I smile at him. And for the first time since this whole mess began with Coach Stennard, one of the guys on the team actually smiles at me.

Maybe church does change people. Felipe sure acted different to me. Or maybe it was Cass that changed him, 'cause Felipe didn't get the bread, either.

CHAPTER THIRTY

THERE WAS SIMPSON SITTIN' OUT IN FRONT of Coach's long driveway. He wasn't there when we left for church, but I doubt it was because he was at church. We had about a foot of snow on the ground, so it wasn't easy for Simpson to get all the way off the road. It was hard not to get a look at his mean eyes. Coach didn't say anything about him, and neither did I, but Megan did.

"Why is that boy always there, Daddy?" she asks.

"Well, honey, he just likes to park his car there," says Coach.

"But why?"

You know this is why adults are adults, 'cause I didn't know any way to answer Megan's question without telling her something that might get her afraid. But Coach did.

"Well, that boy hasn't had an easy life," says Coach. "He's mad a lot. I think he sits out there, at least partly, because he likes to see what it's like to have a family. So he watches us."

"He could come home with us," says Megan.

"He could, but I don't think he wants to be that close to a family just yet, so he watches us."

"Maybe I could pray that he gets a family," says Megan.

"I think that would be a very good idea," says Coach.

You see what I mean about adults. I mean, I would have just said, "Simpson's a creep, and I'm callin' the cops."

"Ah," says Coach, as we pull up to the house, "Snore's here."

There was Snore sittin' in his beat-up gray Nissan.

"Hey, Coach, sorry I'm here early, I got a new song for another dance. I had to come over and see what you think. You know, try it out on you, before I go to Mrs. Pollard."

"It's her say, not mine."

"Yeah, I know, but if you like it, maybe you can talk her into it."

"Well, Snore, I'd love to hear it, but not today. My wife isn't feeling all that well, and I'm afraid I'll have to wait until tomorrow."

"Man, that's too bad. It's a great idea. But I'm sorry to hear about Mrs. O'Connor."

"Thanks, Snore."

"If there's like anything you need, man . . . "

"Thanks," says Coach as we head inside, then he turns to Snore. "Actually, there is something you could do for me."

"Shoot, Coach."

"Well, it would be a big help if you could take Jeremy home. That way I can stay here with Cindy. That okay, Jeremy?"

"Sure," I say, but I think to myself *Do I really want to drive with Snore in that beat-up old Nissan?* "No problem, Coach."

So I get my stuff and jump into Snore's car, which is littered with dozens of CDs, and wrappers from Taco Bell, McDonald's, Wendy's, and Snickers bars, but the car is warm.

"Come on, baby, get us home," says Snore, as we're about to pull out. "She doesn't always like cold weather."

Sure enough, the old Nissan dies just as we lurch forward.

"Temperamental," says Snore.

Click of the key. Nothing. Click again. Nothing.

"Third one's a charm," says Snore.

Click, ppprrrrrruuuurr.

"Ignition. Take off. Take us home, Scotty," says Snore, mimicking Captain Kirk on *Star Trek.*

"Sometimes, when I'm driving along, she'll just

quit for no apparent reason," says Snore, as we pull away from the house.

Not today, I hope, I think to myself.

Snore doesn't really stop when he gets to the end of the drive, just makes a quick left turn and spins his way out onto the road.

"No one's ever on this old road, anyway," he says.

But Simpson is still sitting there near the driveway, and Snore is going just slow enough that I look directly at Simpson's eyes and he smiles at me. But his smile isn't like Felipe's smile in church. I know exactly what his smile means. *At last, I've got him.*

Damn! I think to myself. And then I start praying that this car can get me home, and almost as soon as I do, the car conks out.

"Oh, come on, baby, don't do this to me," says Snore.

Now, I don't know if Snore has seen Simpson pull out or not, but I have, and as the car starts to coast to a halt, Simpson pulls up right behind us.

Click. Nothing. *Click.* Nothing. *Click.* Nothing.

Simpson is walking up to Snore's side of the car.

"What's he want?" says Snore. "Well, maybe he can give us a lift, if the car won't start."

He'll give us a lift, all right, I think to myself. *He'll lift me into the next county.*

Now Simpson's standing right next to Snore's window, which Snore rolls down.

"Hey, Simpson. Car died. Usually starts right up."

"Well, if it isn't Buzza Rat," Simpson snarls, ignoring Snore and looking right me.

Snore looks over at me, then back at Simpson, and back at me. I can see the reality of what is happening spread across his face.

"Get out of the car, Rat!" Simpson says.

I lock my door.

"Get your slimy ass out of the car now!"

With three quick turns of the handle, Snore has closed his window.

"You son of bitch!" Simpson yells, as Snore locks his door.

"Come on, baby, turn over now!"

Click. Nothing. *Click.* Nothing.

Simpson is pounding on the roof and shaking the car. *Click.* Nothing.

Now he's in the ditch trying to find a rock to break the window. *Click.* Nothing.

"This is it, car! Start now or we're all dead!" says Snore.

Click. Click, ppppprruuuuuurr.

What a beautiful sound!

Off we go! Safe.

Thud!

"What the hell was that?!" yells Snore.

"I think Simpson got us with a rock."

"Well, you stupid car!" says Snore, hitting the steering wheel with his hand. "It's your own fault. That's what you get for not starting."

I look at Snore, kind of outta the corner of my eye. I never knew Snore, and now here I am driving home with him, and, in a way, he saved my life. Well, if not my life, a good beating. And, well, maybe, even my life, if I think about it, 'cause I don't really know what Simpson is capable of doing. Snore could have just told me to get out of the car, but he didn't. He didn't hesitate at all. He just rolled up the window and tried to get the car started. Even with Simpson poundin' on the car, he never said, "Get out." Like I said, I don't know Snore well at all. I just thought of him as kind of a goofball who was really into weird music and lights and all that stuff, which meant nothing to me, but Coach saw something in him. Coach really likes him, and he's about as far from a basketball player as anyone could be. In fact, in gym class, kids are always making fun of him. He always gets picked last. With his skinny legs and skinny arms and his long hippie hair and tie-dyed T-shirts and baggy gym shorts, he looks like a rag doll. But Snore did something that not one of those basketball players ever did. He stuck up for me. Big time. And he got a big dent in the trunk of his car for it. And never blamed it on me.

We drive along in silence for awhile, then Snore says, "Hey, Rat, like why is he so mad at you?"

"It's about Coach Stennard," I say.

"Who?"

Like I said before, Snore is so out of touch with school, he's the one person who really doesn't know what's going on.

"The other coach, before Coach O'Connor. The one who tried to attack Cass. The one I had to testify in court about."

"Yeah, yeah. I remember somethin' about that. No, I was just kiddin'. I remember Coach Stennard. One time he made me do like fifty-million jumpin' jacks in gym class because I wasn't payin' attention or somethin'. The guy was a jerk. So he went after Cass. Right. Well, she's a fox, but I wouldn't mess with her."

"Whaddya mean?"

"Cassandra Diaz? Man, she is high class. First, of all she wouldn't give someone like me the time of day. And secondly, I wouldn't want to have to face her old man. He is one mean S.O.B. One mistake with her, and you'd be facing a firing squad."

I've never really heard someone talk like this about a girl. I mean, he just lays it out there. When Snore says that Cass wouldn't be interested in him, it's just a fact. He's not, like, put down by it. It just is. And so he's not interested in her, either. And he's definitely right about her father.

Then Snore smiles at me. "That's why I don't go out with girls for too long a time. Just as soon as I see that's what they're asking me to do—go head-to-head with their old man—I say, 'Why bother?' I haven't found a girl yet that's worth it."

Maybe that's the change in Felipe. Maybe he's willing to go head-to-head with Mr. Diaz. Whoa! He's nuts! What about me? What about Katie? Is she worth that to me? And how would you do that— face a girl's father—anyway?

"Snore, how does a guy figure that out?"

"Don't know. Never done it. I think it has somethin' to do with how you get along with your own father. I think maybe, somehow, your old man— 'cause he's had to do it to get your mom—has some kinda secret to tell you about how to do it. But then, what do I know? I was a kid when my dad left. So I never learned it."

"Simpson was ten when his mom died," I say.

"Yeah, well, mom, dad, it doesn't matter. When you lose one or the other, you get things screwed up," says Snore.

"Thanks," I say, as we pull up to my house.

"Anytime, man."

"I mean thanks for sticking up for me."

"That's cool; 'sides, kids like us gotta stick together."

Kids like us! I think to myself as I walk up the steps. *Kids like us?* Was I like Snore? Was I weird?

Was I really on the outside? Maybe that was the problem. I never, ever thought of myself like Snore. He was weird. Was I weird, like that, too, because of my arm? I knew I was different, and I could see that Snore was different, but were we different in the same way?

CHAPTER THIRTY-ONE

I WENT TO SCHOOL THE NEXT DAY, and the day after, and the day after, and not much changed. Simpson "mentioned" to me a couple of times in the hallway that I was "damn lucky" that he didn't get me that day. He didn't have to tell me that—I already knew it. Snore didn't do so well. Gym class was never easy for him, now it was worse. Simpson decided to wash Snore's hair for him in the shower with his clothes on. One day after school, all four of Snore's tires were flat. Snore never went to the principal, and he never complained. But I think maybe Coach bought him new tires.

We kept winning, easily. We finished the regular season undefeated. Eighteen wins, no losses. I think the closest anyone came to beating us was twelve points. But like I said before, we were expected to win the league championship. Now came sectionals, and maybe beyond.

We were seeded first in the sectional tournament, and we had already beaten the other three Class D teams in the regular season. We won the first game by seventeen points, and the second game by twenty-one. So here we were sectional champions and, for the first time in our history, on our way to the intersectional championship. If we won there, then on to the regionals. And then on to the state semifinals, then the state championship.

The intersectional game was scheduled for Saturday at one of the colleges against a school from Long Island. It was the first day of March, but we had just had a big snowfall, and everyone was hoping the game wouldn't be postponed.

Coach asked me to come over that Friday night to help him get ready for the game on the next day. He wanted to spend some time getting things ready for his wife. He was real nervous about leaving her, because she was getting really close to having the baby. A couple of women from their church were going to come over and stay with her. Coach told me that he had to leave school early and that Snore would drive me over.

"Don't worry, Pat," says Mrs. O'Connor, who was lying on the couch in the living room. "I'll be fine. It's not like I'll be alone."

"Well, I am worried. I've left you numbers where I can be reached, and I've notified the athletic director at the college to get me if you call."

"I'll be fine. Go. Win the game, then I'll have my baby."

"Wait a little longer, Champ, all right?" says Coach, patting Mrs. O'Connor's stomach.

"Snore," says Mrs. O'Connor, "what song are the girls doing this week?"

"A little Jackie Wilson," answers Coach, before Snore can speak. Then he starts to sing,
"'Your love keeps takin' me higher than I've evvvor been takin' beforrror.'"

Then he picks up Megan and throws her into the air.

"'So keep it up. Your love keeps liftin' me, liftin' me, liftin'me.'"

"I hope the cheerleaders dance it better than you do, Coach," says Snore.

"Whaddya mean? Mean I can't dance?" says Coach.

"You ain't exactly, what's his name? That Astaire guy?"

"Don't tell that to my daughter. Okay, Snore, here's the music," says Coach handing him the tape. "You know, the college isn't going to let you do any lights, and you can't bring your whole sound system, but you—Well, I don't need to tell you, you know what to do."

"It'll be great, Coach. Hope you feel better, Mrs. O'Connor."

"I will, soon as the baby comes," she says.

"Not too soon," says Coach.

"He's a nice kid," says Mrs. O'Connor, as Snore hops down the steps toward his car.

"Yeah, he is," says Coach,

"Come on, my little baby, start up," we hear Snore sing as he hops down the porch steps.

"But he better start makin' some money when he gets out of school so he can get a car that starts," adds Coach.

Just then Mrs. O'Connor grimaces.

"You all right?" says Coach.

"Yeah, I think so."

"Was it a contraction?"

"I'm not sure. I think so, but it was different. Oh, my God!"

This time Mrs. O'Connor lurches her head and shoulders forward.

"Oh, my God!"

"Jeremy, call your father, now!"

"Pat! Oh, no. Pat!"

"Cindy, you're gonna be okay."

"Mommy! Mommy! What's wrong? Mommy!"

"Mommy's going to be okay, honey," says Coach.

"Dad! Dad! It's Mrs. O'Connor! Somethin's wrong. Coach, he needs to talk to you."

Chapter Thirty-One

"Pat! Pat!"

"Tell him, it's sharp pains," yells Coach, "like contractions but worse!"

"Dad, you heard? Right. To the hospital, right now. You'll meet us there."

"Okay, let's go. You're gonna have to walk, Cindy. I'll help you. Lean on me. Jeremy, take Megan."

Somehow, one little step at a time, we make it out the door, down the steps, and into the car, and we head down the drive to the road. But right up in front of us is Snore's car. Stopped dead at the end of the drive.

"Won't start again," says Snore.

Coach bolts from his seat. "Get it started and get it started now!" he yells.

"I'll try," says Snore.

"Don't try. Do it!"

By now I'm out of the car, too.

"It's Mrs. O'Connor. She's in trouble," I say slipping through the snow to Snore's window.

Click. Nothing. *Click.* Nothing. *Click.* Nothing.

"Get that goddamned car out of here, now!"

"I'm tryin', I'm tryin."

Click. Click. Click. Click. Click. Nothing. Nothing. Nothing. Nothing. Nothing.

"I'll push it out with my car."

"You can't, Coach. It's stuck in park. It won't move," yells Snore to him.

Then Coach looks up, and there, standing about twenty feet away like a hyena stepping from the woods drawn by the smell of the blood of a fresh kill, stands Simpson.

"What's the matter, Coach," he says, and I watch that grin of his spreading at the corners of his lips. "You got problems?"

CHAPTER THIRTY-TWO

"MY WIFE'S GONNA HAVE HER BABY," says Coach matter-of-factly. "Snore's car won't start."

"Too bad," says Simpson.

"Simpson, I've got to get her to the hospital now."

"Like I said, too bad."

"You don't understand, she's sick. If she doesn't get to a hospital, she's gonna die."

Simpson doesn't say anything to that.

"Simpson, what do you want me to do? You want me to beg you? I'll beg you. Simpson, I beg you. I need your car. You want me to say I'm sorry, then I'm sorry. Forgive me, I was wrong. I'm at your mercy, Simpson. She's gonna die."

"Pat! Pat! God help me! Pat!"

"Please, Simpson!"

"Mommy! Mommy!"

"Simpson, you've got to help," pleads Coach, and then he pauses and adds, "Please, for your mother."

"You leave my mother out of this, you bastard!"

"I can't Simpson, I need your help. You know your mother wouldn't want you to turn your back on us. On my little girl. You wouldn't want her to grow up without a mother, too, would you?"

I don't know what Simpson planned on doing when he first walked over to us, but now it was clear he had to make a decision, and fast. He looked at Coach, at the car, at me, and at Snore, and I could see all of these things happening to him in seconds. This isn't what he expected. This isn't what he wanted. This isn't how he thought he would get his revenge. It had all spun out of control. He had to decide!

"How we gonna get her to my car?" he finally blurts out. "There's no place to walk because of the snow."

"I don't think she can walk. We're gonna have to carry her," says Coach.

"All right. All right. All right! Then let's carry her," says Simpson.

"Thanks," says Coach.

"I'm not doin' this for you," says Simpson. "I'm doin' it for the kid."

"Thanks, anyway."

Now the strangest thing happened with

Simpson. It was like all that anger got turned into doin' somethin' right. And like I said about him being strong as a moose, well, that was sure what we needed, because with all that snow on each side of the drive and the bushes and trees, it wasn't gonna be easy to get her to Simpson's car. We could barely get the door of Coach's car open, and then we had to get past Snore's car.

"I'll come in the other side, and we'll slide her out of the seat and then, Simpson, can you get her when she comes out your side?"

"Yeah, I can take her under her arms," says Simpson.

"Okay, we'll go slow, slow. You got her, Simpson?"

"Yeah, I'm okay."

"All right, I'm comin' around, and I'll support underneath her. Snore, you get one leg, and Jeremy, you get the other. Jeremy get on the side that's your good arm, so you can hold. Don't worry, Cindy, we got you. Megan, you just stay here until I come back to get you."

"I don't know if I can hold her," I say, as we inch our way through the snow toward Simpson's car.

"Rat, you better hold her. You've got to hold her," says Simpson to me.

And so I tighten my grip, and then I realize that Mrs. O'Connor is holding my hand. My bad hand. Tight. I don't remember anyone holding my ugly withered hand, like it was a real hand—maybe my mother did—but I don't remember it. But it was a real hand to Mrs. O'Connor.

"I'll sit in the back with Cindy," says Coach, once we get to Simpson's car. "Jeremy, go back and get Megan and sit up front with her on your lap. Snore, you're on your own. Simpson, go fast, but be careful."

So we speed down the road, Mrs. O'Connor tryin' to muffle her groans, Simpson checking his rearview mirror each time she did, and Megan cryin' with me tellin' her not to.

Dad was waiting at the emergency room with a bunch of other doctors and nurses.

"Okay, get her on the stretcher and check the vital signs now. How often are the pains coming?" he says to Mrs. O'Connor.

"Every minute or so," she says.

"Contractions?"

"Not like contractions. Worse," she says.

"Doctor," says one of the nurses, "we've got blood."

"Okay, let's get going. This is going to be a C-section, Pat. This isn't an option," says Dad, as they wheel her down the hallway. Dad doesn't look at me or Simpson. He doesn't even know we exist. And I guess that's the way it should be.

We watch them race through the doors that say "No Admittance," and now I'm standing in the waiting room with Megan and Simpson.

Chapter Thirty-Two

"Your old man's somethin'," says Simpson.

I look over at Simpson, and I nod, but I can't help but think, *How weird is this? Standing in a hospital room, listening to the guy who hates me the most in life talking about how he admires the guy that I think I hate most in life. And the guy I admire most in life, Coach O'Connor, is the guy he hates most. I mean, that's strange.*

Then it occurs to me that Megan is standing there holding my hand, and I haven't once thought about her, so I look down at her. She's holding Simpson's hand, too.

CHAPTER THIRTY-THREE

IT'S ABOUT MIDNIGHT WHEN DAD comes out. Megan is sound asleep on my lap. Simpson's sitting next to me like a zombie. He never said a word the whole time we sat there. He only got up once to move his car out of the emergency area. The two women from the church had stopped by to find Snore still stuck in the driveway, so they're sitting in the waiting room, too. And Snore had finally gotten his car going and he's sitting next to Simpson.

"Well, Mrs. O'Connor had a baby boy—Raymond Patrick O'Connor," says Dad.

And I know why they named him Raymond, I think.

"How's Cindy?" asks one of the women from church.

"She's not out of the woods. She lost a lot of blood

188

and she was weak from the illness," says Dad. "But there are some good people watching her." Then he turns to us. "Pat told me what happened out there. You guys did a good job. You should be proud of what you did. All of you." Then he looks right at me. "All of you."

You know hate is a strange thing. And so is love. I can't help it! I do admire him! Simpson's right. He's a great guy. It means a lot to me to have this guy tell me that I did a good job. He doesn't say that to just anyone, or for just any reason. And he said it to Snore and Simpson and me. I would have jumped up and hugged him just then, but Megan was on my lap so I didn't. Or couldn't. Or wouldn't.

After he left, I thought about what just happened with him and me. That's what love is. That's what love feels like. It explodes inside you like some beautiful flower that blooms in your heart all at once. But hatred? Hatred sits there and waits until you're alone and quiet and then it seeps back into your heart after the love has exploded and faded from memory. So the moment passes, and the hatred comes back. I wish I could stop it, but I can't. I can't forgive him for not wanting me. I just can't. Or is it that I won't? Now there's an interesting idea. This love and hatred thing: Is it a choice? My choice?

"What illness?"

The voice was Simpson's.

"What?" I say.

"Your father said she had an illness," says Simpson in a dull, flat voice. "What illness?"

"She has cancer," I say.

Simpson kind of grunts, nods his head a little, and then I see a tear start to form in his eye like the first drop of water from a rooftop icicle in early spring.

"Cancer," he whispers. "What kind of God is there that lets people get cancer?"

Now he's cryin' for real, and me and Snore have no idea what to do. So one of the women motions to Snore to let her sit down next to Simpson. And soon enough, he's bawlin' on her shoulder like a little kid. Simpson, big, mean, awful, dumb Simpson, cryin' like I used to when kids made fun of me because of my arm. I'd run home to my mother, because I couldn't stand the pain of thinking that they liked me, and then out of nowhere one of them saying something like, "Don't get too close to his ugly arm, or you'll get it, too." Then the teasing: "Weird arm. Weird arm. Cooties! Cooties!" And so I'd run home, crying. But at least I had a mother to cry on. Simpson never did.

Dad must have called Mom, because she showed up after a little while. She invited Simpson and Snore to come to our house. Simpson just said, "No," and Snore said he had to check his sound system for the game. The game. In just a few hours we would be playing some team from Long Island for the chance to advance toward a state title. You know, all night long, I hadn't once thought about the game. I bet you Coach didn't, either. And I knew that when we played, Coach wouldn't be on the bench.

CHAPTER THIRTY-FOUR

"JEREMY, CHECK AND SEE IF IT'S ALL RIGHT for me to go in?" says Mrs. Pollard.

"Hey, guys," I yell into the locker room. "Mrs. Pollard wants to know if it's okay for her to come in?"

"Everybody dressed?" yells Felipe. "Tell her it's okay."

"Well, I'm not going to pretend that I know what I'm doing out there," she says. "You guys know what to do. Obviously, this is a good team you're playing; otherwise they wouldn't be here. Just do what you know how to do."

It seems to me like someone should say something like, "Any word on Coach's wife?" but no one does.

Or someone should say, "Hey, Mrs. Pollard, can we, like, say some kind of prayer? You know, not to win, or anything, but for Coach and his wife?" But no one does.

And Mrs. Pollard would say, "That's a good idea. Why don't we all get in a circle, and say something to yourselves that makes sense." But she doesn't say that, and we don't pray. I think maybe those things only happen in movies.

I don't say it, either. I don't bow my head and close my eyes. Maybe I'm wrong, but I can't bring myself to ask God for anything then. I just don't know how to pray that way—like on demand. When I think of something, well, then maybe I'll ask God. Maybe I'll remember later to pray for Coach and his wife. Maybe the fact that I even think about it is a kind of prayer. Maybe by thinking about it you wake up a little to the fact that you're supposed to pray, and maybe that's what prayer is.

This team from Long Island looked fast and they looked like they could jump. I know we had never met a team this good, probably not since the school in New Brunswick. I just hoped the result wasn't the same, 'cause those guys whipped us bad.

The other team won the tip and scored on a quick lay-up. Ryley brought the ball up court and called the defensive set that we would run if we scored. He tried to throw the ball in to Greg at the high post. But the defenders were all over him, and Greg lost the ball. Two-on-one fast break, and it was four nothing. Second time up the court and Ryley tried to force a bad pass to Niko at the other high post. Another fast break, and it was six nothing. Josh got careless on the inbound pass to Ryley. They stole the ball. Eight nothing.

"Time out," yells Mrs. Pollard to Felipe.

"What are you doin?" Greg yells at Ryley, as they head to the bench.

"Whaddya mean me? You gotta help out," says Ryley.

"Where the hell is your head?" says Felipe to Josh.

"I didn't see him comin'," says Josh.

"You're supposed to see him," says Niko.

"All right you guys, be quiet, all of you!" says Mrs. Pollard. "I'm not your coach, but I've coached enough games myself to know that you're not working together. This is the first time all year that you've met a team that's as good as you. Now you're gonna have to work, and you're going to have to work together. Stop the bickering! Work your plays. Do what you've been doing all year long. Now, come on, let's go!"

They stopped bickering, but they didn't have a lot of success. It was like the other team knew exactly what we were running—on offense *and* defense.

Just before the first half ended, I saw Simpson walk into the gym. I thought he might come to the game, but I really didn't know what to expect from him now. As we headed toward the locker room, down by fifteen points, Simpson walked across the court toward me. And just as he got to me, who should run out toward the court for their dance routine but the cheerleaders. And like three cars crashing into one another at a street corner, me and Simpson and Cass run smack into one another.

Simpson looks at Cass, and I can see a look of fear and disgust on Cass's face as she steps back to go around him. He looks right at her.

"Sorry. I'm sorry."

I don't know if he means for running into her or for everything he's done. And she sure doesn't know. And I'm not sure if Simpson even knows.

"I mean, I'm sorry. Really sorry."

So I guess he does know.

Cass just looks at him, and then says, "I gotta go cheer."

Then Simpson turns to me. "I gotta talk to the guys."

"Whaddya mean, Simp?"

"I mean, I gotta talk to them, right now. There's somethin' I gotta tell them."

"Well, I don't know—"

"Please, Jeremy, I'm tellin' you, I gotta talk to them."

I don't think Simpson has ever called me Jeremy in his life.

"Okay," I say. "Come on."

And there I am standin' in the locker room, listening to all the guys yell at each other, and then one by one they turn and look at me and Simpson. And then it's all quiet.

"What's he doin' here?" says Niko.

"Simpson's got somethin' he wants to tell you," I say.

"Tell him we ain't interested in anything he has to say," says Ryley.

"We got enough to think about," says Jordan.

"Whaddya bring him in here for anyway, Rat?" says Greg.

"Yeah, Rat, what the hell are you doin', anyway?" says Niko.

"He asked me—" I start to say, but Simpson interrupts me.

"He's doin' me a favor," he says. "I gotta talk to you guys. I—I need to tell you somethin'."

Silence.

"I'd give anything to be playin' with you guys—"

"Big deal! You blew it a long time ago," says Greg.

"I know it. I did . . . but, well . . . the thing is . . . you're not gonna win tonight."

"This is what you came to tell us!" yells Ryley.

"Get the hell outta here!" says Greg.

"No! No! Let me finish!" says Simpson. "You're not gonna win—if you keep doin' what you're doin."

"What are you talking about?" says Mrs. Pollard.

"They know your plays," Simpson blurts out.

"Whaddya mean?" asks Ryley.

"They know everything you're doin'," says Simpson.

Quiet.

"How?" asks Mrs. Pollard.

Simpson looks down at the floor. "I got in touch with some of their players. I sent them a playbook," he says.

"You son of a bitch!" yells Felipe. "I shoulda beat the crap out of you when I had the chance."

"Simpson, how could you?" says Mrs. Pollard.

Simpson looks up. "Well, I could. And I did. And it's over, but you can't win if you keep doin' what you're doin'. You gotta try somethin' different."

"Well, that's great," says Felipe. "We don't have a whole lot of *different* things to choose from. The last I looked, this is what we got."

"Well, not quite," says Simpson.

"Oh, great, the traitor has an idea," says Ryley.

"Well, I do," says Simpson.

"Why should we listen to you? You're only gonna go tell them," says Greg.

"I know you shouldn't trust me—"

"You're right, we don't," says Felipe. "Now leave."

Simpson just stands there for a long moment.

"Leave," says Niko.

"I trust him," I say.

"What!" says Felipe.

"I said, 'I trust him.'"

"Well, who gives a crap about you!" says Greg.

One kick in the stomach too many!

"None of you bastards! That's for sure! Why should I bother caring about you or your stupid game. You don't give a damn about me, or about Coach, or about his wife, or anything! All you care about is winning, and here comes a guy who swallows his pride and walks in here to help you, and you don't even care about that. So the hell with your stupid game and the hell with all of you!"

Silence. Long silence.

"Two minutes," comes a voice through the door.

"What's your idea?" whispers Mrs. Pollard, turning to Simpson.

"It's the last page of the playbook," says Simpson, excitedly. "When all else fails: Have courage! Take a risk! Be creative!"

"That's it?" says Ryley.

"Yeah, that's it," says Simpson. "Don't you get it? Do what they don't expect."

"Yeah, but what?" says Niko.

"Go back to what we used to do. You're the best three-point shooters around. Sit outside and shoot, and then press the hell out of them for the rest of the game."

I could see the guys start to realize that this

might just work.

"It's not a bad idea," says Mrs. Pollard.

"It's worth a chance," says Ryley.

"Might just work," says Felipe.

"Once they come out to guard us, then we can run the motion offense," says Greg.

"Okay, let's give it a try. You've got nothing to lose," says Mrs. Pollard.

I open the door, letting in the sounds of the cheerleaders dancing to "Your love keeps liftin' me higher, than I've ever been lifted before."

They rush from the locker room.

"Liftin' me, liftin' me."

And there I am standin' with Simpson again, but this time there's no Megan in between us.

"Keeps liftin' me higher."

Finally, he looks at me, "You're somethin', kid. Just like your old man."

"Higher and higher!"

CHAPTER
THIRTY-FIVE

RYLEY HIT THE FIRST THREE, and we stole the ball on the next two inbound passes that they tried. So we were down by eight. They finally got the ball up court, but missed their shot. Greg took the next three-pointer, and we were down by five. Now they called a time out.

They didn't think we'd keep bombing the threes, but Ryley, Greg, Niko, Josh, and Leduane kept shooting and hitting.

It was almost the end of the third quarter before they adjusted to our three-point offense, and now we were up by six. Once they switched from their three-two zone to a man-to-man defense and came out to guard against the outside shot, we were up by nine. And then we started to run the motion offense. We were up by fifteen. It looked like we were on our way to the regional championship game!

Chapter Thirty-Five

The buzzer sounds! Game over! Snore turns on his sound system to the Jackie Wilson song; the cheerleaders are clappin' their hands and dancin'. Everybody's jumpin' all over the guys on the team. I'm so happy we won, I mean real happy, but then I look over at Simpson, who isn't jumpin' up and down.

"Look at that asshole," some kid says, motioning with his head toward Simpson. "I'll bet you he's sorry he quit."

Yeah, I s'pose he is, I think to myself. *But not the way you think.*

Simpson's eyes are red and glazed over. And there's my father standing next to him. I start to walk toward them, but suddenly Simpson turns and walks out the door.

I know what to expect. I can see it in my father's eyes. Simpson had the same eyes. Eyes that can't hide what they know.

"We won," I say sheepishly, like somehow by saying 'We won,' I would hold back what is about to happen.

He nods at me.

"Mrs. O'Connor," he begins, then swallows hard.

"Dad—"

"She didn't make it, son."

I bury my head into his big chest wanting everything to stop. Just stop! No game. No basketball. No

Simpson. No Coach. No Megan. No Mrs. O'Connor. Nothing! Nothing! Nothing! Just stop! Stop it all! But it won't stop. It can't stop. It just keeps coming. Life. Death. Being kicked in the stomach. Again, and again, and again. What's the use. It just keeps coming at you.

"Too much," I hear Dad say, "too much for her."

One by one people break off from the celebration, and they see me crying. And one by one they look at Dad, and he tells them the same thing. And one by one they realize that Mrs. O'Connor is dead. One by one they think about Coach and Megan and just-born Raymond. One by one they see how absolutely stupid this game is.

It means everything and it means nothing, I say to myself.

Now I know the nothing part.

EPILOGUE

ARE YOU LOOKING FOR A HAPPY ENDING? They don't come that easily. We didn't win a state championship. No one was really into the game. Guys tried to get up for it; they'd say things like, "Let's win this one for Coach," who wasn't there. But it's a strange thing; you can't pretend to do somethin' for someone else, if you don't really want to do it. It's like, well—you figure it out.

Coach didn't come back to coach or to teach. He decided to move down to New Brunswick to be near Ray and his wife, who could care for the kids. But before he left he called me up and asked me to come over.

"Can you come in, too?" I say to Dad, as we pull up to the house.

"You want me to?"

"Yeah, I don't know if I can do this alone."

"Hey, guys," says Coach. "Come on in. You remember Ray, right, Jeremy?"

"Yes, sir," I say.

"Ray, this is Jeremy's dad, Dr. Chandler, who stayed with Cindy throughout . . ." Coach can't quite finish that thought. "And this is Ray's wife, Yvonne. Glad you could come. I wanted to say good-bye to you in person, Jeremy, and I know Megan did, too. Meg!" he hollers.

Megan comes running in with a present in her hands.

"It took me awhile before I could go through Cindy's things, like the paintings that were so much a part of her," says Coach, as he tries not to cry. "She had been working on one that you had inspired, Jeremy. Cindy was very fond of you, and I know she would like you to have this," he says and now he is crying. "It wasn't all finished—she didn't have time."

"Go ahead, Jeremy, open it," says Megan.

So I open the package, and there is a painting in a gold frame of a holy-looking woman, standing on a hill, watching over sheep. It's done the way the other paintings—the icons—are painted. Flat, no emotion, but her eyes look right at me.

"It's really nice," I say, but I can't figure out why they gave me this. I only went to church with them once. But then I notice the holy woman's right arm. It's withered.

"Read the inscription," says Coach.

"St. Germaine Cousin, 1579–1601," I say out loud. "Born with a withered right arm."

I look up right into Coach's eyes.

"A withered right arm," says Coach, "and a heart filled with courage. Don't ever let anyone call you 'Rat' again."